'Why did you if you were not

Dante knew he was bombarding her with questions, but he couldn't help it. It alarmed him immensely to think that she had no one else to voice concern over her well-being.

'Because I have to earn my living, that's why!' She hadn't meant to shout, but anger helped Bliss to hold back the more powerful underlying emotion that was threatening to engulf her. A need for Dante to hold her, to cradle her against that comforting hard-muscled chest of his was growing inside her at such a rate as to scare her witless. What was she thinking of? Did she imagine for one second that he would welcome such a display of feminine weakness? He'd probably run a mile if he thought she needed him in any way, let alone if he found out she was pregnant with his baby!

But he mustn't find out.

The day **Maggie Cox** saw the film version of *Wuthering Heights*, with a beautiful Merle Oberon and a very handsome Laurence Olivier, was the day that she became hooked on romance. From that day onwards she spent a lot of time dreaming up her own romances, secretly hoping that one day she might become published and get paid for doing what she loves most! Now that her dream is being realised, she wakes up every morning and counts her blessings. She is married to a gorgeous man, and is the mother of two wonderful sons. Her two other great passions in life—besides her family and reading/writing—are music and films.

Recent titles by the same author:

THE ITALIAN'S PREGNANCY PROPOSAL

BY
MAGGIE COX

MILLS & BOON®

First published in Great Britain 2005
Harlequin Mills & Boon Limited,
Eton House, 18-24 Paradise Road, Richmond, Surrey TW9 1SR

© Maggie Cox 2005

ISBN 0 263 84163 4

Set in Times Roman 10½ on 12 pt.
01-0705-53376

Printed and bound in Spain
by Litografia Rosés, S.A., Barcelona

CHAPTER ONE

BLISS knew she really ought to resist, but she couldn't help stealing another surreptitious glance at her watch to check on the time when her dragon of a supervisor's back was momentarily turned. The store was hot and crowded and the overpowering scent of perfume from the counters arranged around hers was making her feel as though she'd wandered into an opium den. Besides that, her eyes itched from the shadow she was forced to wear to promote the make-up, and she longed to be able to scrub it off along with the foundation cream, blusher and lipstick that transformed her into someone she almost didn't recognise. It was too bad she'd have to endure another two hours of this torture before she could give in to such a rebellious desire.

What on earth she'd been thinking of when she'd decided to work in the plush department store that catered mainly to fashion-conscious women with more money than sense, she didn't know. Well, yes, she did know. She'd been between jobs yet again and as inspiration about what she really wanted to do had been in appallingly scant supply, she'd let her best friend Trudy persuade her to apply for a post in the same store that she worked in. For Trudy, who loved all things retail, it was heaven. To Bliss, it was increasingly turning out to be just the opposite.

'Excuse me… I would like to purchase a lipstick.'

'Certainly, madam. Do you have any particular shade in mind? I can show you the— Oh, Lord!'

Bliss watched in alarm as the striking brunette in front of the counter slid weakly down to the floor, almost like a slow-motion replay of an actor fainting in a soap opera. Beside her, an apple-cheeked toddler with big brown eyes and curly dark hair ensconced in a pushchair cried out in distress. Her actions automatic and concerned, Bliss flew round the counter to crouch beside the woman who had passed out, at the same time taking a brief moment to stroke the baby-soft cheek of the toddler and murmur something soothing. A small crowd quickly gathered and Bliss took immediate charge, urging them to stand back while she loosened the collar of the woman's silk shirt beneath her expensive suede coat, then gently smoothed back the wavy dark hair from her olive-skinned forehead.

'I don't... I don't feel well.' Momentarily the woman's surprisingly blue eyes fluttered open and her lush mouth trembled slightly as she stared dazedly up at Bliss. 'Look after my baby,' she said beseechingly in her accented voice before she fainted dead away again.

'Don't worry. I will.' Her teeth clamping down worriedly on her soft lower lip, Bliss glanced across at the now-quietened toddler, who stared back at her with wide-eyed interest, as if wondering what might be going to happen next.

'Now, what's happened? Do you know this woman?' Her supervisor pushed her way through the small knot of curious bystanders and knelt down beside Bliss in anxious distaste—as if she really didn't need or want this untidy disruption to her working day. Fighting down the little spurt of annoyance that burst like a bubble inside her chest, Bliss briefly shook her head.

'She's a customer and she's just passed out. We're going to need an ambulance; can you organise it? Oh, and can somebody please get this little girl a drink? She looks hot. Hardly surprising when there's enough heat in this place to compete with the inside of a volcano!'

After that, things happened fairly quickly. It seemed a mere matter of moments before the familiar sound of an ambulance siren wailed in the distance, then came to an abrupt halt outside the store's entrance. Having checked the woman had no foreign objects in her mouth, was still breathing normally and was as comfortable as she could make her, Bliss was relieved to have the two highly competent ambulance men take over. Remembering her promise to the child's mother, Bliss took charge of the toddler in the pushchair, fed her a drink in a plastic lipped cup, then, when she began to whimper at the surrounding mayhem, lifted her out of the pushchair and safely into her arms for a cuddle. One of the ambulance men glanced over his shoulder at her as he and his colleague lifted the unconscious woman onto a stretcher.

'That her child?' he asked.

Bliss nodded. 'I've got her bag too.' She grabbed up the expensive-looking tan leather shoulder bag she'd thrown onto the empty pushchair for safekeeping before someone either squashed it underfoot or, more worryingly, absconded with it. 'It might have some ID inside it.'

'You'd better bring it along with the child. You can ride in the ambulance with the mother. What's your name, love?'

'Bliss Maguire.'

'So you're Irish like meself?'

'Half,' Bliss muttered, thinking it was bizarre to be having such a conversation about roots under the circumstances. 'On my father's side.'

'Ah, well, we'll get along just grand, then, you and I.'

With a teasing grin, the man turned his concentration firmly back to the woman on the stretcher.

It soon became apparent that the child needed to eat. After informing the nurse behind the hospital desk that she was going to the canteen if anyone should come looking for her, Bliss followed the arrows to the dining area. Glad that she'd had the foresight to bring her purse with her before getting into the ambulance, she purchased a sandwich and a cup of tea, then sat at a corner table with her charge on her lap, feeding her small bites of bread, cheese and cucumber. By the obvious eagerness with which she ate, it was clear the little girl was ravenously hungry.

'Probably all the excitement,' she said out loud, 'poor lamb.' Her heart turned over in sympathy for both the child and her mother. Being separated from each other in such an unexpected and frightening way must be torment. She could only pray that the woman would make a speedy recovery. She also hoped that her next of kin would arrive soon to look after this beautiful child and give her the opportunity of seeing a familiar face. Momentarily Bliss rested her chin on the silky dark head, laughing when the little girl handed her a piece of soggy sandwich, the child watching entranced as Bliss began to chew with exaggerated emphasis to amuse her.

'Miss Maguire?'

She glanced up at the accented enunciation of her name into the glittering green-eyed gaze of the most stunning-looking male she'd ever seen outside the pages of a high-fashion glossy magazine. She'd once glimpsed a well-known Hollywood movie star shopping with his entourage in the store, but even he—noted heartthrob that he was—couldn't hold a candle to this particular male specimen. As her gaze skimmed over his gleaming, slightly longish black hair, then helplessly detoured to take in a tall, well-muscled frame dressed in the kind of clothes that gave off an aura of comfortable wealth beyond what most people could possibly dream of, her heart felt in danger of going into arrest, so violently did it jolt.

'Who wants to know?'

Unconsciously protective of the beautiful child in her arms, she tightened her hand round the tiny waist in her pretty velvet dress. Silently she vowed that she would not be handing her over to anyone without the right credentials as verified by the proper authorities…no matter how well dressed or impossibly handsome he was.

'My name is Dante di Andrea. I am the brother of the woman you accompanied in the ambulance to the hospital. The child you are holding is Renata Ward—my niece.'

The child gazed blankly up at the man, with no discernible sign of recognition. Bliss felt something in the pit of her stomach tighten warily.

'Really?'

The handsome brow crinkled with annoyance. 'You do not believe me?' He looked as if the mere idea of anyone disbelieving anything he said was tantamount to gross bad manners or derangement on their part. *How dare you question my authority?* his emerald eyes silently blazed.

'Why would I lie about it? Come, Renny. I will look after you now.'

'I'm afraid I can't just hand the child over to you just like that.' Affecting her best 'head girl' voice, Bliss ignored the outstretched arms of the dark-haired pin-up in front of her and dared to meet his disbelieving glare with a decidedly cool and firm one of her own. 'We'll go back to Casualty Reception and I'll ask them to verify that you are who you say you are.'

'Your diligence is commendable, Miss Maguire, but how do you think I came to find you if my credentials have not already been verified by the proper authorities? Did you speak to my sister before she passed out? If you did, you must know from her accent that she is Italian, like me. My name and cell phone number were in her purse; that is how I come to be here now.'

All that might be so, Bliss thought defiantly. But she still wasn't taking any chances. She was more unwilling than she could have believed to release the little girl into anyone's arms but her mother's. She'd never forgive herself if anything untoward happened while this precious child was in her care.

'I did speak to the lady before she fainted, and it's because of that that I am going to double-check you are who you say you are.'

'What did my sister say to you?' Clearly struggling with his temper, Dante di Andrea narrowed his sizzling verdant gaze on Bliss like a sniper about to take a pot shot at a target he detested, and scowled.

'She told me to take care of her baby and that's exactly what I'm doing.' Rising to her feet with 'Renny' now snuggled up tiredly against her chest, Bliss tried not to be intimidated by the fact that the man hovering over the pair of them like some royal bodyguard was at least a good six inches taller than she was. In fact he made her average height seem positively short.

'So…we will return to Reception and we will speak to someone in authority who will assure you that I am Dante di Andrea, the brother of Tatiana Ward, and then you will hand over my niece to my care. *Sì?*'

Feeling her face flame red as his furious glance swept

almost dismissively across her features, Bliss bit back an equally provoked retort and decided to say nothing. The last thing anyone needed was a row under the circumstances. All she wanted to do was make sure that Renata would be released into safe hands. Holding the child tight, she strode into the long corridor outside the canteen ahead of him, secretly wishing that the man had not been quite so speedy in his arrival at the hospital as he had. Renata smelt so sweet, was so snuggly, warm and delicious in her arms, that all Bliss's usually determinedly buried maternal instincts were given full and free rein to an almost alarming degree.

'I can definitely assure you, Miss Maguire, that Mr di Andrea is indeed the brother of Mrs Ward who is at present undergoing observation by the head doctor on duty. The little girl is his niece, Renata Ward.' The very efficient-looking middle-aged receptionist with her steel-framed spectacles and ash-blond hair smiled patiently at Bliss as though she were addressing a confused child.

'Oh.' Bliss's violet eyes blinked twice in succession, as though she'd just been rudely woken from a peaceful slumber. She heard the harshly relieved breath that Dante di Andrea released beside her before holding out his arms once again for the little girl. The provocatively sensual scent of sandalwood floated up to her nostrils as he did so and something in her deepest feminine core reacted as violently as though he'd kissed her. 'Your uncle will take you now, sweetie. Be a good girl, won't you? You'll see Mummy soon.'

It was the oddest thing, but Bliss suddenly felt as if she might burst into tears. What stopped her was the fact that Renata had started to cling to her in alarm when Dante had reached out, making little sounds of protest against Bliss's white silk shirt that tore at her heart as powerfully as any heartbreak could.

'All right, honey…all right. There's nothing to be frightened of, I promise.' Except that when Bliss's accusing stare met Dante's across the little girl's dark head, the sheer frustration and rage in his eyes made her doubt that promise greatly. Something told her in that short, unsettling exchange that this was a man unused to being defied in any way, and so far Bliss had not capitulated to his authority one iota. Her wild imagination suggested he looked about ready to tear her limb from limb.

'Give me my niece, Miss Maguire. I thank you for taking care of her in her mother's time of need, but now I want to go and see my sister and I would like to take her daughter with me.'

'She's acting like she doesn't know you.' It was hard to believe the strength with which Renata was holding onto Bliss's shirt, her little chubby fists clinging on as though her life depended on it. Did her uncle have to look quite so fierce? That scowl would put the fear of God into a wild cougar! Maybe his anxiety for his sister was putting him under a strain, but he could soften a little for the child's sake, couldn't he? 'How am I supposed to hand her over to you when she clearly doesn't want to go?'

He cursed beneath his breath in a barrage of fluent Italian. Even the outwardly unruffled receptionist looked alarmed. But Bliss was adamant that, however effusively Dante di Andrea gave way to temper, all it would achieve would be to make her more determined not to hand Renata over until he had calmed down.

'The baby is very shy and not used to me.' Shaking his head, he seemed to suddenly struggle with finding the right words, as if he wasn't used to having to explain or justify his emotions. Against her will, Bliss couldn't deny the spurt of sympathy that bloomed inside her. 'She has recently lost her father. That is why Tatiana—her mother—is ill.'

Bliss went very still. Sensing the change in her posture, Renata glanced up into her eyes, her bottom lip quivering. 'I'm very sorry to hear that. Look, Mr di Andrea, I'm not trying to make things difficult for you. I just want to make sure that the little girl is all right…for my own satisfaction, you understand?'

For a very surreal moment, Dante was so drawn by those ravishing violet eyes with their curling sable lashes that he forgot he usually concurred with his father's view that the English were a cold race. The warmth and concern that this unknown Englishwoman was expressing for a total stranger's child took him aback and made him reassess his former prejudice in a way that was definitely unsettling.

'Perhaps we should sit down for a moment, *sì*?'

They moved to a long bench seat a little way off. When Dante sat down beside her, Bliss couldn't help feeling slightly overshadowed by his awesome male beauty and she withdrew her gaze to the child because focusing on that remarkably handsome visage was making it almost impossible to concentrate.

She'd heard it said that an Italian man's face told the story of his life. If that was so, Dante di Andrea had a lifetime of experience and confidence and knowing written across his. Along with his smooth bronzed skin and piercing green eyes, he had an allure that could captivate a woman in an instant, and no doubt an inbuilt arrogance that he took as his God-given right. Yes, Bliss had already seen ample signs of that arrogance. She sighed.

Renata was asleep. When Bliss experienced the full

weight of that little warm body sagging against her, she capitulated to an instinctive urge to smooth those whisper-soft curls away from her velvet forehead, then planted a tiny kiss on the child's dampened cheek. If she didn't hand her back to her intoxicating uncle very soon, Bliss would be in danger of being charged with kidnapping. Why did her maternal instincts have to kick in now with a child who was completely unrelated to her? Why couldn't they have waited until she was in love and expecting a child of her own? Feeling an almost overwhelming upsurge of emotion inside her, she swallowed to ease the sudden painful cramping in her throat. *Where is your head, Bliss Maguire? You know that will never happen!*

'What happened to your sister's husband…if you don't mind me asking?'

Dante didn't want to talk about that now. The pain of Tatiana's loss was so great that it had affected every one of them like the aftermath of an earthquake. Dante, his brother Stefano, and their parents, Antonio and Isabella— they were all disorientated, like shocked survivors dazedly picking over the remnants of what used to be their homes. One minute Matt Ward had been celebrating a considerable promotion at work, and the next he had been ploughed down by a drunken driver while on his way home to Tatiana and his baby. *Il mio Dio!* His baby sister had been so happy and in love.

Dante had been envious of the joy she had found with the young Englishman, and considered it highly unlikely that he would ever find the same joy with a woman. Not when his considerable fortune and dedication to his work threw up obstacles that seemed insurmountable. Dante wasn't interested in women who were attracted by his wealth and position as head of the family business. But it seemed gold-diggers were the only type of women who came into his sphere. It had made him wish sometimes that he could have been as carefree as Tatiana, allowed to come to the UK to study and live an ordinary life that didn't require great responsibility and the level of commitment that Dante had had to contend with. But now he had no cause for envy, only pain and regret that the great happiness Tatiana had enjoyed had been cruelly snatched away and this lovely child would never know her father.

As he momentarily dug his fingers into his brow to try and stifle his distress Dante was startled to feel the consoling press of the Englishwoman's hand through his suit sleeve. Along with the scent of vanilla and honey, her touch sent ripples of seductive sensations along his already highly sensitised nerve endings.

'You don't have to tell me,' she said softly. 'You must be anxious to see your sister. Here, take the baby. She's asleep now.'

Wordlessly Dante took the child, tucking her in close to his broad chest in his exquisitely designed jacket and shirt, feeling his heart swell at the soft, warm body and dreading the anxiety on his sister's face when he appeared at her bedside. Tatiana had always been so open and so trusting. Now her joy in life was gone. Dante longed for a way to bring it back.

Suddenly distracted by a pair of shimmering eyes the astonishing colour and vivid hue of violets, he willingly focused all his attention on the beautiful girl seated beside him. Her white silk blouse was damp and crumpled at the front where Renata had lain her head against her chest and her rich black hair was slipping strand by silky strand loose from her pony-tail. The hotly sensuous charge that surged through his body like a streak of sultry summer lightning as a result of his intense examination was too disturbing for words.

'*Grazie*. I was told that you work in the store and that you travelled in the ambulance with my sister. You must allow me to pay for a taxi so you can return.'

'I can get myself a taxi, but I really don't want you to pay.' Bliss got to her feet and, disturbingly, Dante did likewise. As he towered over her once again she couldn't help feeling consumed by his presence. The man was so attractive and so impossible to be ambivalent towards that it wasn't funny. To counteract the effect, she deliberately focused all her attention on the sleeping child in his arms, secretly thinking that they made a touching tableau—the handsome, indomitable uncle and his beautiful baby niece. It cut her to the quick to realise she would probably not set eyes on either of them ever again.

'At least leave me your address, Miss Maguire. My sister will no doubt want to get in touch with you to thank you for all your help.'

Bliss shrugged to hide her sudden awkwardness. 'She doesn't have to thank me. It was my pleasure to be able to help. If I want to ring and find out how she's doing, it's Mrs Ward, isn't it?'

'Tatiana.'

'What a lovely name.'

'And Bliss? Where did that come from?' Raising one dark eyebrow with an almost roguish air, Dante smiled. A wave of heat sailed through Bliss's body and back again.

'Maybe it's what my parents were looking for at the time.' Her deadpan humour clearly didn't amuse him. His raised eyebrow was replaced by a distinct frown.

'*Felicità.*'

'Pardon?'

'That is "Bliss" in my language. *Felicità*. But I think I prefer it in English.'

Oh, my Lord! Do you have to smile at me like that? Bliss felt as if she'd been locked in a pitch-black room only to be let out blinking into the blinding gaze of the sun. What on earth was God thinking of when he made a man as devastatingly irresistible as Dante di Andrea? What he'd said was perfectly innocent, but in that sexy Italian intonation it had sounded to Bliss as if he were making love to her with words. Crossing her arms in front of her shirt, she anxiously strove to conceal the fact that her nipples had shockingly peaked to shameful steel buds inside her bra and the sharp tingling sensation that ensued in them was almost bordering on pain. 'Well. I wish both you and your sister and little Renny all the best. I'll be going now.'

'Your address, Miss Maguire. Please?' He'd juggled the child against his chest and produced a small notepad and pen from his inside jacket pocket. Wordlessly Bliss took it and scribbled down her address and phone number, though it was only after she handed back the notepad that she wondered why she'd capitulated so easily. She'd told him thanks weren't necessary and she'd meant it. Now she'd gone back on her word and maybe Dante would think that she expected something because of it? She hoped not. She'd hate him to imagine that she'd helped his sister in the hope of some kind of reward.

'Well…goodbye.'

With an awkward little smile that a shy teenager would surely have despaired of, Bliss allowed herself one final glance at the stunning Italian and the equally beautiful little girl, then turned and walked quickly away towards the double-doored exit.

CHAPTER TWO

ALTHOUGH Bliss was convinced that the repetitive ringing sound that permeated her subconscious was a referee
blowing the half-time whistle on a soccer match, it
quickly transformed into the more insistent peal of a ringing telephone, and she rubbed at her eyes and dazedly
sat up in bed. Reaching for the cordless receiver on the
small oak cabinet beside her, she stifled a yawn before
uttering a weary 'yes' into the mouthpiece.

'Bliss Maguire?'

All drowsiness was banished in an instant and her violet eyes pinged wide open. If she wasn't mistaken, that
deeply knee-trembling pronunciation of her name belonged to the Italian hunk she'd met yesterday in the
hospital. Dante di Andrea. Pushing her fingers shakily
through her hair, Bliss concentrated hard on getting her
jaw to work in order to reply. 'This is she.'

'It is Dante di Andrea speaking…you remember?
From yesterday at the hospital?'

Did she remember? She'd replayed their meeting over
and over in her head like a videotape stuck on rewind.
Especially when she'd rung the hospital only to be told
that Tatiana Ward had been discharged to go home and
was not being admitted as an in-patient or even trans-
ferred to a private hospital.

'I remember.' Somehow her voice had acquired a disturbingly husky quality and Bliss coughed a little to clear
her throat. 'Excuse me,' she quickly apologised. 'I found
out that your sister was sent home. How is she today?'

'*Depressa ed afflitta.* I am sorry…depressed and heart-sick. I have ordered her to stay in bed for today. She has not been getting a lot of sleep lately under the circumstances. That is why she passed out in the store. Her husband died only six weeks ago and she is finding life very difficult at the moment.'

'I'm so sorry to hear that.'

'Can we meet?'

'I beg your pardon?' Her heart had started to throb alarmingly and Bliss wondered for a moment if her brain were so addled, she'd simply misheard him.

'I will be blunt with you, Miss Maguire. My sister needs some help. Matt—her husband—had no living parents and until my mother can get here from Italy again, she will be on her own with Renny and myself. I have taken some time off from my business to be with Tatiana, but I am no expert with children and until she fully recovers, she will need some help taking care of my niece.'

Pushing up the defiant shoestring straps on her silky cotton nightie, Bliss took a few moments to absorb what he was saying, surprise and trepidation vying equally for precedence inside her chest. Where was this leading? Was he asking her to come and help take care of Renata? Did he not realise she already had a job? Of course he did! He knew she worked at the store where his sister had fainted, which was how she had come to be at the hospital in the first place.

'Mr di Andrea, if you are asking what I think you are asking, I'm afraid it's impossible. Much as I think the little girl is utterly adorable, I have to work for my living. If your sister needed some help in the evening I might be able to—'

'If you come and stay with Tatiana and Renny for a while until my mother comes from Italy, I will pay you a more than generous fee for your services and the disruption to your schedule. If your place of work will not grant you time off, then I will endeavour to acquire a better position for you somewhere else. I have lots of contacts in the business world, Miss Maguire. It will not be difficult.'

Bliss didn't doubt that he had contacts, and that he could get her any job he damn well pleased. One brush with Dante di Andrea's confident, self-assured persona and you knew straight away that he was a man who could move mountains if he had to. But did she really want to give up her job and her livelihood on the word of a man she had only just met, albeit only briefly? If things didn't work out she could always temp, she supposed. She was used to using temporary work as a fall-back when things didn't turn out as she'd hoped. If she was honest, retail really wasn't her thing anyway, and if push came to shove she had just about enough money in the bank to tide her over for a very short while until she found another position. Her palm felt clammy where it clung too tightly to the phone.

'You said "stay" with your sister. Could I not just come over in the mornings and stay until the evening, and then go home?'

'Since her father has been gone, Renny wakes in the night sometimes. Tatiana is not in a fit state to see to the child properly on her own. Therefore it would be best if you packed a few things and came to stay indefinitely.'

'Mr di Andrea…this may sound obvious, but have you thought about approaching a child-care agency for help?'

'I do not want a stranger taking care of my niece!' came back the vexed reply.

Puzzled, Bliss frowned. 'But *I'm* a stranger. You only met me yesterday, remember?'

'I could tell from the moment I saw you with her that you are a person my niece feels drawn to. Because you comforted her yesterday, she will remember you.'

'But she didn't seem to remember you, if you don't mind my saying.'

There was a harsh indrawn breath at the other end of the phone. 'I have not spent a lot of time with Tatiana since she had the child and therefore, yes…I am a virtual stranger to Renny. I have been busy with my business in Italy. Yesterday was the first time we were together since the funeral a month ago. I had to return almost immediately to Milan, along with my parents. My father is not in good health himself and my mother worries about leaving him on his own. None of us like the fact that Tatiana has basically had to cope with this tragedy by herself and I am working on finding a solution to that, believe me. In the meantime, until my mother can arrange acceptable nursing care for my father and travel to England, Renny and Tatiana need all the help I can provide for them.'

'So you want to know if I will help?' Shoving off the mulberry-coloured duvet, Bliss restlessly swung her legs off the edge of the bed and pushed her feet into her sheepskin-lined moccasins, still holding firmly onto the phone.

'*Sì*. Will you help us, Miss Maguire…Bliss?'

He really didn't have to ask again because Bliss had already made up her mind to accept the task. And if they made things difficult for her at the store to take the time off, she would see it as a clear sign that she really wasn't meant to be there in the first place. God only knew what she *was* meant to be doing and she hoped that one day soon she would get a clue. In the meantime she would look forward to seeing the adorable Renata again. And if her thoughts leaned longingly towards seeing her handsome uncle again as well, then Bliss made no apology for that.

Tatiana Ward lived in a ground-floor apartment in Chelsea Harbour. When Dante had given her the address, Bliss had sucked in her breath and released a long, low whistle. It was a location that had at least a million-pound price tag just to sniff the air in that hallowed place—never mind live there! Thinking of her own one-bed flat in a notoriously run-down area, Bliss was suddenly struck with trepidation at the idea of accepting this unexpected job of nanny to a little girl whose connections were clearly in a different stratosphere from her own humble origins.

Bliss's parents had never had much money. Her mother had suffered from serious bouts of depression all her life that had impeded her ability to work, and when Bliss was just sixteen her mother's depression had finally shockingly driven her to take her own life. With her father already drinking his own life away, Bliss had gone out to work at sixteen to help support the two of them, but one day not long after her eighteenth birthday he had packed his bags and gone. He'd left no forwarding address, just a scrappy little note saying he was sorry for not turning out to be the father Bliss deserved and begging her not to try and find him. She'd long ago decided she had to make some sort of shaky settlement with her devastating past, but situations like the one she now found herself in were apt to test that decision to the hilt where her self-confidence was concerned. Her childhood had been an unmitigated disaster and nearly every memory she had of it hurt.

Now standing outside the front entrance to the apartment in Chelsea Harbour, Bliss determinedly reached down inside herself for some fresh courage, flicked an imaginary speck of dust from the sleeve of her short leather jacket, then, without further ado, pressed the button on the intercom.

'*Ciao!*'

'Mr di Andrea? It's Bliss Maguire.'

'Wait a minute, will you?'

Even though he'd answered the intercom, she was unprepared for the sight of Dante di Andrea with a serious-faced toddler hoisted on his hip, answering the door with what looked like a very strained smile. Noting some kind of cereal congealing on the front of his beautiful white shirt where the lovely Renata had obviously decided to share her breakfast with her uncle, Bliss seriously struggled to prevent the twitching of her lips into becoming a full-blown grin. She was pretty sure Dante would not appreciate it. But even though he was a little less than immaculate this morning, with his arresting green eyes and darkly brooding male beauty, the man could still engender a small riot of appreciation from the opposite sex just by walking down the street.

'Hello. Clearly a fan of oatmeal, I see. Shall I take her?' Adjusting the strap of her bag on her shoulder, Bliss reached out for Renata. When the child willingly went into her arms, Dante murmured something in Italian that could have been either surprise or relief or both. 'Come in, Miss Maguire. You have not arrived a moment too soon.'

The apartment was lovely—flooded with natural light, with maple wood floors and some very tasteful antiques that Bliss knew would have to look out once Renata really started getting into her stride. Leading her to a pair of long low leather couches with a glass coffee-table with wrought-iron legs positioned between them, Dante bade his visitor sit down. 'I will change my shirt, then I will be back.' With a wary glance at the little girl who was coiling her chubby fingers into Bliss's shoulder-length dark hair with obvious fascination, he went out of the door again and left them alone.

Bliss occupied herself with amusing the child while she waited for Dante to return, her heart rate a little calmer now that she didn't have to contend with glancing into those daunting green eyes. Lifting Renata onto her hip, she strolled across the wide expanse of beautiful maple floor to the window, gazing out at the vista of yachts and cruisers bobbing on the water with a soft sigh of appreciation.

'What a lovely view you have, Renny. Aren't you a lucky little girl?' Then immediately remembering that the child's father was dead, Bliss silently cursed her own tactlessness. But Renata was smiling up at her with those big innocent brown eyes, totally unaware of any dilemma, her chubby cheeks dimpling adorably as Bliss smiled back at her. Unable to resist, Bliss dropped a small butterfly kiss at the side of her pretty rosebud mouth and sighed.

'It was good of you to come, but where is your suitcase? I understood from our telephone conversation that you were coming to stay.'

He was sporting another immaculate white shirt with his tailored black trousers, his dark hair glistening with blue-black lights as fiercely as a midnight sky with the light of the moon reflected on it. Looking vaguely perplexed, he focused his gaze with concern on Bliss.

'I thought I'd bring my things over later. I wanted to come and talk to you first about the…about the arrangements.' Her voiced trailed off because she was suddenly struck by acute self-consciousness in the intimidating presence of Dante di Andrea. Much more so than she had previously anticipated. She'd dressed in well-worn jeans and a fitted black tee shirt beneath her leather jacket— casual clothes she was comfortable in—only all of a sudden she had doubts about what was expected. Was she too casual? In view of the effortlessly stylish and handsome man in front of her, she couldn't help but feel decidedly underdressed. Scruffy, even.

Dante was silently casting his eyes over Bliss's considerable slender curves in her tight jeans and tee shirt, musing that she resembled a young Claudia Cardinale with her wide-spaced brows, beautiful eyes and unknowingly sexy smile. For a moment her beauty distracted him. He wouldn't be true to his blood if he didn't notice and appreciate a beautiful woman, but it had been a while since he'd experienced the fierce heat of arousal simply by gazing at one. Sensing the smouldering fire of attraction stirring in his loins as he stared at her, he thought how soft and inviting her rich dark hair looked floating loose against her shoulders and how much he would enjoy the privilege of touching it and letting it slide through his fingers.

'I didn't know…wasn't sure what to wear. I'm probably unrecognisable without all that make-up, aren't I? It's unfortunate, but they make you put it on with a trowel if you work on the beauty counter. I can't wait to take it off most days.'

As Bliss's almost breathless voice petered out Dante forced himself to concentrate his thoughts more appropriately. He couldn't afford to start lusting after the woman he had reached out to for help with Renata and her mother, no matter how aroused she made him feel. That would not be appropriate at all under the circumstances. He was a businessman, a hotelier with a respected reputation, and he wanted to show this young Englishwoman that she could trust him when he was around her.

'You look fine.' He wanted to tell her that beauty like hers would win her many admirers even without the dubious aid of make-up. In the end he curtailed his natural inclination and decided not to make things more awkward by complimenting her. As a result his tone was perhaps more curt than he meant it to be. 'I am learning that one cannot be concerned about protecting one's clothes when there is a little one around. The more casual you are, the better.'

'You're right.' Smiling back at him, Bliss couldn't deny her relief. She wasn't exactly looking for his approval of her appearance, but it was nice to know that he didn't think it might mean her level of commitment was as casual as her clothes. 'Would you like me to clean her up? Wash Renny's face and hands for her?'

'I will show you to a bathroom.' Dante's smile was brief and all too quickly gone. Once more Bliss detected strain behind the gesture. It reminded her of the reason she was there. 'How is your sister today?'

'She is sleeping right now, because she did not have a good night. She was restless with weeping.' His bronze skin seemed to turn momentarily pale and Bliss experienced an unexpected tug on her heartstrings. 'The doctor is coming out to her in a little while to give her a checkup. When you have cleaned up the baby we will talk business, *si*?'

Sensing he was much more comfortable with discussing something of a less personal nature than his sister's well-being, Bliss followed him out into the corridor and into an exquisitely marbled bathroom that looked as if it belonged to some Hollywood movie star instead of a young, recently widowed single mum. Gesturing towards some shelves stacked high with perfectly folded, freshly laundered white towels, Dante lingered in the doorway as Bliss ran hot and cold water into a marble basin with Renata happily chattering baby talk into her ear.

'Everything you need should be here. If there is something you cannot find, just ask.'

He seemed to hesitate as his glance drank his fill of the charming picture of tender domesticity that she and his niece made together, and Bliss felt her cheeks suddenly burn beneath his unsettling scrutiny. 'What is it?' she asked, violet eyes wary.

'You are so natural with the baby. I am thinking that you perhaps grew up with lots of brothers and sisters, *sì*?'

'No.' Smiling as she dipped a face-cloth into the warm water, then squeezed it out, Bliss sat Renata down on the high chrome stool beside the sink and carefully and lovingly started to clean up the little girl's breakfast-stained face. 'Just the opposite, in fact. I'm actually an only child. I've just always loved children.'

'But you are not married?'

'No.' Briefly glancing up at the frown currently drawing his dark brows together, Bliss shook her head. 'And neither do I intend to be. Marriage doesn't interest me much, Mr di Andrea. As far as I'm concerned all marriage does is engender false hope in a happy outcome that very rarely manifests itself.'

Dante's frown grew even more pronounced. 'So you would have children out of wedlock?'

Clearly recognising that he disapproved of such a course of action in a big way, Bliss couldn't help laughing. 'That's probably not on the cards either. I shall just be happy being auntie to my friends' children.'

He murmured something with feeling, in Italian, and Bliss glanced up at him reprovingly as she finished cleaning Renata's face. 'You'll have to remember that I don't speak Italian. I wish I did, but I don't.'

'Forgive me. I just said that it was a terrible waste that a woman with such natural maternal instincts should look forward to a life without a husband and children of her own.'

'Well, that's as may be, but I can assure you that nothing would induce me into marriage.'

'That is a pity.' His eyes darkened as Dante reflected that it truly was.

'You are not married yourself, Mr di Andrea?'

'Dante.' Her question was so surprising that for a moment he struggled to marshal his thoughts together on the subject. The fact that his mother had been berating him for his single status for so long now came back to remind him what a disappointment he must be to her on that score. Business-wise he was one of the élite of Italian hoteliers, adding to the family fortune year by year with his natural and almost frightening ability to make money—but personally…? While his younger brother Stefano—his right-hand man in the business—had already fathered three children and had been married for almost eight years now, and Tatiana of course had Renata, Dante was still a confirmed bachelor with not a prospect of a *bambino* in sight. And nor would there be unless the most exceptional woman came along—one whose first interest wasn't in how much money he had.

'No, I am not married. I am—how do you say it?—married to my business.'

'Oh.'

Just, 'Oh.' Not, 'What do you do?' or, 'What business are you in?' Just, 'Oh.' Did he hold such little appeal to this surprising woman that her curiosity wasn't even provoked the smallest bit about what he did for a living?

Her attention already straying to a still-chattering Renata, Bliss drained the water from the basin, rinsed it out with some cold, then lifted the toddler cheerfully onto her hip again. For some reason that he couldn't quite explain, Dante's proud male ego felt ridiculously bruised.

'All done. We can have that talk now, if you like.'

He nodded gravely. '*Sì*. If you come into the kitchen I will make some coffee for us. You have eaten breakfast, I presume?'

'I had a cereal bar on the way over here. I never eat much in the morning.'

'That is not good. Eating should not be such a casual affair.'

'Of course, you would say that. You're Italian, aren't you?' Her prettily shaped mouth curved into a playful smile as Dante scowled and he experienced the full force of her teasing with a wave of heat that frankly stunned him.

'By that you are implying what—that we eat too much?'

'No.' Reining in another teasing smile, Bliss carefully weighed up her words. 'I just meant that food is a big part of your culture, isn't it? Food and family and…' She was just about to add 'love' when she saw the corner of Dante's too-appealing lips quirk upwards into a lazily amused smile. She was dumbstruck; her gaze was helplessly hypnotised by that sensually stimulating little gesture, so much so that a deliciously affecting shiver shuddered down her spine like little sparkles of coloured light shimmering from a firework.

'*La dolce vita.* A love of life, *sì*?'

The way he said it sounded too sinful for words and Bliss couldn't help musing that he was the epitome of all the things Italian men were renowned for and more. Sexy, stylish, charming, strong, definitely arrogant and jaw-droppingly beautiful...

'Yes. That's it.' Embarrassed at being caught staring, she slid her violet gaze guiltily away. When Dante smiled at her again as if he knew exactly what she was thinking, Bliss wished the floor would open up and swallow her.

'Come and have some coffee and some food, then we will talk.'

He turned his back on her and left the bathroom, his tall, broad-shouldered frame moving with a lithe grace that beautifully complemented the undoubted strength in every taut and sinewed muscle that rippled beneath his shirt. Bliss could only trail behind in awe.

'So, we have an agreement? You will go back home and collect your things and stay here with Renata and my sister until my mother arrives from Italy.'

'As long as your sister is in agreement that I stay in her house and help take care of Renny. If she is, then, yes, I agree to stay.'

Dante sighed as if a huge weight had been lifted from his shoulders. Glancing towards his little niece, who was playing with some crayons and paper on the floor, his green eyes turned visibly soft. 'It is bad enough she has lost her father, no? And now her mother cannot take care of her.'

'But this is only temporary,' Bliss hastened to assure him. 'Tatiana will recover soon, I'm sure.'

'Yes, you're right.' If he was honest, Dante was very glad to have Bliss to talk to. There was an air of calmness and maturity about her that was very appealing and right now he needed that. He prided himself on his efficiency and aptitude in almost every other arena of his life except personal relations. There was always a discernible distance between himself and his parents and siblings, no matter how hard he tried to let his guard down. It had been that way since he was small—because his mother Isabella was not his natural mother.

Dante had been the result of an affair his father Antonio had had with an Irish girl whom his father had been forbidden by his own parents to marry. She had died of breast cancer shortly after giving birth to their child. Heartbroken, Antonio had broken all allegiance to his parents after Katherine died and looked after his baby son himself with the aid of his sister-in-law Romana, until he had met and married Isabella Minetti when Dante was six years old. A year later, Stefano had been born, followed only eighteen months after that by Tatiana. Isabella had never treated Dante any differently from his brother and sister, yet Dante had always felt somehow cheated because he wasn't her natural-born son. Particularly so when his aunt Romana had often reminded him that it was his fault that Antonio and his parents were not speaking any more. She had also reminded him, on an almost daily basis, that he was lucky to be even tolerated in the family because of what had happened, and behind his father's back had sneered at him, 'Irish brat.'

If Antonio had guessed what had gone on when he was out at work trying to get his business off the ground, Dante had no doubt his father would have taken him from Romana so fast her head would have spun. But Antonio had never known what his sister-in-law was truly like, because Dante had never told him.

When the boy Dante had finally found himself with

two loving parents, he had still felt himself an outsider—always the one with something to prove. It had been easiest to concentrate all his energies on the business. But now his sister had suffered this terrible tragedy and there was a real opportunity to demonstrate his allegiance and his love, and do everything in his power to help Tatiana. Perhaps it would help him let down a few of those painfully erected barriers he'd built so diligently round his heart…with his sister, at least.

'This afternoon if Tatiana feels like talking, I will take you in to see her yourself. Perhaps she will open up a little to another woman? My mother rings her every day, but it is not the same as having her here with her, is it?'

'No, it isn't,' Bliss agreed, her heart full at the troubled expression crossing Dante's extraordinarily captivating face. Her own relationship with her mother had never been as close as she would have liked it to be, but she could certainly understand Tatiana's sense of loss at not having her mother nearby under the circumstances. 'But I will gladly talk to Tatiana if you think that might help. By the way, don't forget to leave me your telephone number so that I can contact you when you leave.'

Dante's green eyes glimmered a little as he treated Bliss to the full, unsettling force of his concentrated gaze.

'That will not be necessary,' he said curtly.

'Why not?'

'Because I am staying here as well. I thought you realised that?'

CHAPTER THREE

IT WAS a possibility that had not even remotely crossed Bliss's mind. Now her thoughts culminated in a crescendo of panic as heat cascaded through her body like a sudden tropical storm, battering down defences and raising unbidden fears about sleeping under the same roof as this breathtaking, beguiling Italian. She desperately wanted to help Tatiana and her lovely little daughter— of course she did—but that desire was now complicated by the fact that she was starting to harbour what could only be ultimately a futile attraction to Dante himself. It was so unlike her to react like that to a man—*any* man, no matter how attractive. Now this out-of-the-blue, violent attraction for one who was practically a stranger was enough to make her question her own reason.

Seeing the startled look in her pretty eyes, Dante sensed her mind working overtime. He realised that there were things he hadn't said. Important things that she should know about him so that she would be reassured that this wasn't some elaborate game he was playing to take advantage of her in any way. With a gargantuan effort, he dragged his gaze away from the sweetly perfect curve of her hips highlighted by her tight denim jeans as Bliss stood up from the kitchen table with Renata in her arms, holding the little girl close as her head drooped tiredly against her shoulder.

'It is natural you should be wary, but I need to stay here so that I can keep an eye on Tatiana and the baby. My family would never forgive me if anything should happen to either of them. *I* couldn't forgive myself should such a terrible thing occur.' He too got to his feet, towering above Bliss from the other side of the table so that she had to look up to meet the fiercely protective blaze in those breathtaking eyes of his. 'I do not know how to handle a small child such as Renny. I am too inexperienced. I am not a family man in the sense that I have a wife and children. That is why I need your help, Bliss. My brother Stefano and I are hoteliers. As well as hotels in Italy, Sardinia and Paris, we have a small select hotel here in London, in Belgravia, where we have a suite in readiness for whenever the family should visit. But I do not want to stay there while my sister is clearly in need of my help. Please tell me you understand my dilemma?'

Bliss let out a breath and her previously tense shoulders dropped a fraction. Dante di Andrea was clearly an extremely wealthy and attractive man with a strong sense of familial duty and love. It was totally absurd to imagine that he would be remotely attracted to an ordinary, unremarkable girl like her and put them both in a compromising position when she was only there out of the goodness of her heart. Anyway, he probably had a string of gorgeous girlfriends back in Italy—each of them no doubt more beautiful than Aphrodite herself. *Oh, well, Bliss, you can breathe a sigh of relief. He won't be lusting after you the minute he sees you in your chain-store dressing gown.* The thought made a severe dent in her ego, even though it was absolutely ludicrous to entertain it in the first place.

'It's all right, Mr di Andrea.'

He immediately frowned and she quickly realised he wasn't entirely happy with her formal use of his name. 'Dante.' Despite feeling that addressing him informally was a liberty that was far too intimate, Bliss rallied. 'I'm cool about the situation if you are. As soon as your mother gets here from Italy I'll go home and that will be that. Right now I'm just glad to be able to help out. The little darling's asleep. Can I put her down somewhere?'

'Of course.' Swiftly moving ahead of her into the living room, Dante cleared some cushions from one of the stylish leather couches and indicated to Bliss that she should lay the sleeping child there. When she had done so, he fetched a soft crushed pink cashmere throw from an armchair and draped it tenderly over the little girl. Watching the look on his face as he did so, Bliss felt her heart swell with warmth. He wasn't experienced with children, he'd said—yet he gazed at Renata as though the miracle of her existence touched him to the very depths of his soul.

'I think I'll take the opportunity to go home now and fetch my things. Can I phone for a cab from here?'

'That will not be necessary. I have a driver at the hotel who will come and pick you up and take you home. I will ring him now and he will be downstairs in just a few minutes. Please do not be long. If you are too long I may fear that you are not coming back at all.'

The way he said this made Bliss feel as though she had just agreed to a secret tryst with him in the moonlight. His tone held a surprisingly possessive note that made all the fine hairs on the back of her neck sit up straight. How was she supposed to maintain a very necessary emotional distance from this man when such a riot of forceful feeling was flooding through her? She had to get a grip, that was what she had to do, and remind herself that she was here to do a job and that was all. There was no place in her life for futile crushes or romantic attachments of any kind.

Bliss might not be sure exactly what she wanted out

of life, but she was certain of one thing—it wasn't a relationship. Experiencing the tragedy of her parents' marriage at first hand, seeing two people who'd started out loving each other withdraw into their own private hell, unable to even care for their child because they were so wrapped up in their own misery, Bliss had seen just how bad relationships could get. Who needed the heartache? Her mission right now should be to focus on her career and stop going down old roads that held no prospects and no opportunity of improving her situation.

'My bag is already packed. All I have to do is pick it up and bring it with me.' Although her voice was even, her gaze pulled away from Dante's with more difficulty than he would ever know.

When she returned in the black limousine that had been her ride back to Chelsea Harbour, Dante led Bliss straight into the living room where Renata was seated on a cushion in front of the big wide-screen television, watching children's programmes. Catching her completely unawares with a guilty but lethally sexy grin, Dante shrugged his magnificent shoulders and dropped his hands to his tight lean hips. 'We have been watching cartoons together. Such a simple pleasure, but one I have been enjoying immensely. It is a joy to spend time with my niece and have the pleasure of hearing her laugh. It is the best thing that has happened to me in a long time.'

She felt like a ninepin just knocked down by a bowling ball. For several seconds Bliss could do nothing but stare at him. Her jaw went slack, and her rising sense of panic made her seriously wonder if he'd put her into some kind of trance, because she couldn't have torn her gaze away from the joy in that beautiful face if someone had paid her with gold bars. With his strong, accentuated jaw line, straight, aquiline nose, a mouth that hinted equally at arrogance and strength and now humour, and those intensely disturbing emerald eyes, his sensual power alone packed such a punch that Bliss was amazed she was still standing. Team such a weapon with his clearly passionate kinship to his sister and her little daughter and—well, resistance was useless, wasn't it?

'Spending time with children, sharing the kind of things that they enjoy doing…it can remind you of what it was like to be a child.' Dropping her leather holdall onto the maple wood floor, Bliss smiled up at him, thoroughly disconcerted when his expression seemed to grow more serious and his eyes all but made a meal of her on the spot. That look wasn't anything to do with memories of being a child. On the contrary, it was a look that was everything to do with a virile adult male at the height of his sexual prowess, and who could blame Bliss for feeling as if she'd mentally been stripped naked by an expert?

'You brought your things, that's good. Come, I will show you where you will sleep tonight.' Dante broke away before Bliss did, his manner suddenly abrupt and businesslike, and she was left staring at his back as he exited the room, her heart pounding. In fact it was pounding so hard that she told herself she was *this* close to needing medical help. Irritated with herself for behaving so completely out of character around an attractive man, Bliss combed her fingers impatiently through her hair, took a deep breath, picked up her bag and obediently followed him out into the light airy corridor, warning herself to pull herself together as she did so.

'Chocolate, yummy.'

Back in the living room a few minutes later, Bliss lay

on the floor with Renata seated astride her chest, dropping chocolate buttons one by one into her laughing mouth. Dante had disappeared somewhere else in the apartment to make some phone calls, he'd told her, and so for now at least Bliss could relax. She was having fun with her small charge, relieved to be spending her time playing rather than working at a job she'd rapidly been growing to hate, and worrying about what she was going to do next.

When she experienced a sudden tingling of awareness at the back of her neck, she realised that she and Renata were not alone. Quickly pushing up into a sitting position, she clasped the child firmly around her small waist and smilingly declined any more chocolate buttons. Then she gave her small charge a peck on the cheek and rose carefully to her feet, taking the little girl with her. Leaning an arm against the doorjamb, Dante stood in silent contemplation of them both.

'You might have indicated you were there!' Bliss said accusingly, unsettled by the fact that he'd been watching her when she hadn't known it. Seemingly unconcerned by her outburst, Dante parted his lips in a surprisingly unperturbed smile.

'Bliss, do you not know that to deny an Italian male the opportunity of gazing at such sublime beauty is like starving a deep-sea diver of oxygen?'

Her embarrassed blush the same eye-catching hue as raspberry jam, Bliss took refuge in the sweet baby scent of the toddler in her arms rather than concentrate her attention on her uncle. 'Yes, the baby is lovely. Of course you're allowed to gaze at her. When she grows up she's going to be a real heartbreaker, aren't you, sugar? I only wished you'd warned me you were there. You took me by surprise, that's all.'

'I did not just mean the baby.'

This time Bliss did drag her gaze back to Dante and as his words lit up her insides like the fifth of November she silently warned herself of the folly of being flattered by them. Dante was Italian. Italian men were famous for their flirting—they learned it at their mother's breast. He was only doing what came naturally and probably acted the same with all women whether they were nineteen or ninety. She most definitely shouldn't take it personally.

'Anyway…you look like you wanted to tell me something.' Anxious to change the subject, she jiggled Renata up and down against her hip, deciding to concentrate purely on the child and only speak with Dante when she absolutely had to. That way he would see that she was completely professional about the job he had hired her to do and would not be seeking to ingratiate herself in any way with him.

'I thought you might like to come in and say *ciao* to Tatiana. She is awake and wants to see you and little Renata.'

Relieved more than she could say for such a timely intervention, Bliss nodded immediately. 'I would like that very much. Thank you.'

Tatiana Ward lay propped up against a pile of crisp white pillows, her shoulder-length dark hair left softly loose around her shoulders. Her face, devoid of make-up, was pale and fine-boned, her riveting sapphire eyes commanding both admiration and attention in their jewel-like intensity. As Bliss followed Dante into the lovely room with its calming décor and riverside views she saw Tatiana pull up the embroidered cream counterpane over her blue silk nightdress and knew that she wasn't the only one who was nervous about being introduced.

Murmuring something in Italian for his sister's ears alone, Dante leaned across to place a small kiss at the side of her head and Bliss saw Tatiana reach out briefly to squeeze his hand as if to thank him for his support. Then she lifted her gaze to Bliss and held out her arms for her little daughter to come to her.

Bliss immediately passed Renata over, taking the bag of chocolate buttons and laying them on the lacquered Chinese cabinet beside the bed, her heart swelling at the sight of mother and child holding each other close. Then, almost shyly, Renata pulled away to sit up in her mother's lap, grinning disarmingly up at the new female who had appeared in her life.

'You are very kind to help me, Bliss. When I saw you behind the beauty counter I thought to myself that you had a kind face. *Compassionevole, sì?*' She glanced at the tall, commanding figure of her brother standing beside the bed as if searching for confirmation.

'*Sì.*' Dante disarmed Bliss with a studied little smile. 'Compassionate.'

'I was glad to help. Please, think no more of it. How are you feeling today?'

'Tired. I cannot seem to get my body to do what I want it to do. You must think that I am not a very good mother, Bliss, when I cannot even care for my little one.'

Her brilliant blue eyes clouded over with despair and tears quivered on her curling dark lashes like crystalline pearls. Not giving her actions a second thought, Bliss dropped down on the side of the bed beside Tatiana and gently stroked her arm. 'You are grieving, Tatiana. You have every right to feel tired and depleted and that certainly doesn't make you a bad mother! All you need is some tender loving care and some time to heal. I will stay and help as long as you need me—that's a promise.'

'*Grazie.* I am very lucky to have found you. It is clear my daughter is quite at home with you. It does my heart good to know that.'

At that moment, Dante was privately echoing his sister's feelings on the matter. When he saw Bliss reach out to comfort his sister, as if giving solace to others was a natural and integral part of her make-up, he couldn't stem the tide of pleasure and need that pulsed through him at the sight of her small, perfect hand against Tatiana's arm. So much so, he almost wished it were him she was administering to. What was it about this pretty English girl with her mercurial violet eyes that tugged on his affections and desire more than any woman he'd known in ages? He'd barely been acquainted with her for five minutes and yet he was craving her attention like a love-sick teenager pining after the prettiest girl in the classroom. With a colossal effort he banished such thoughts as well as he could, knowing his first priority was to his sister and her little daughter. As soon as his mother arrived from Milan, Dante would go back to his work and put every thought of the arresting Bliss Maguire far from his mind.

But as Bliss returned to the living room later on that evening after bathing Renata and putting her to bed Dante's hungry gaze followed her slim, denim-clad figure with unapologetic thirst, a quiet but explosive tension criss-crossing his taut midsection and making his body too unsettled to sit. Her feet were tantalisingly bare and the sweet tip-tilted curves of her breasts beneath her tight black tee shirt were all too evident to his appreciative male gaze. As she moved fluidly across to one of the couches, picked up a satin cushion and sat down with it clutched to her chest Dante was perturbed at how forcibly desire banished every single thought in his head except his very primeval need to make love to her.

'Your niece is fast asleep. Poor little thing just couldn't stay awake. Don't worry if she wakes in the night—I'll easily hear her from the room next door.'

For a long moment words were a commodity that Dante could no longer count on. Her eyes were so ravishing and her voice so soft that he was caught up in the spell of her. Pushing out of his chair, he stood by the armchair he had just vacated, the tension in him totally annihilating the possibility of keeping still right then. *Mamma mia!* What was this woman doing to him? He had hired her to help with Renny—not become an object of his suddenly unquenchable lust!

'Dante?'

'I hope she will not wake and that you will get a good night's rest. I have become only too aware that looking after children is very tiring. In a good way, of course, but still tiring.'

His concern warmed Bliss more than it had a right to. 'It must also take a lot out of you, doing what *you* do.' Her interest in this man overriding her vow to keep as professionally distant as possible, she hugged the cream satin cushion to her breast and waited for him to answer.

'Being a hotelier is not hard.' Shrugging one wide muscular shoulder beneath his white shirt, Dante didn't seem to consider it to be that big a deal. But running, not just one, but several international hotels must require a lot of business acumen as well as flair and dedication, Bliss imagined. Either he was being overly modest, or he simply had so much talent and ability that he didn't view problems in that arena as other people might. Observing the coolly self-possessed and confident demeanour he presented, Bliss had no doubt it was the latter.

'My father bought the lease on a hotel when I was only small. He worked hard to make it a success and eventually was able to buy it outright. By the time my brother Stefano and I were grown, he owned several other hotels as well. It was really not so difficult to join the business and help increase its success.' What Dante didn't reveal to the interested young woman seated on his sister's couch was that when he had first stepped in to join his father, Antonio had already lost two of his hotels in investments that hadn't come off and had been close to losing another. After studying accountancy and business management on a part-time basis in the evenings as well as learning the business firsthand from his father, Dante had acquired a distinct flair for doing exactly what was required to turn things around. In less than two years after he had officially started working with his father, they had not only regained the two hotels they had lost, but acquired another two as well. By the time Stefano had come along to swell the ranks, the di Andrea hotels had gone from strength to strength, earning an international reputation for first-class service and what Antonio proudly called 'old-fashioned style and comfort'. The customers were always right and nothing they required was too difficult or impossible to get. With such a motto, as far as Dante was concerned, they could not lose.

'And do you enjoy your work?' Bliss wanted to know.

'I am passionate about it.' One corner of Dante's intriguing mouth lifted ever so slightly at the edges as if he was amused she even had to ask such a question.

Bliss couldn't help but sigh enviously. 'I wish I could find a job or career I was passionate about.'

'You do not like working behind the beauty counter?'

'Are you joking?' She made a face and moved the satin cushion to one side. 'Sometimes I think I'd rather dig roads! At least I'd be out in the open in the fresh air instead of almost choking to death beneath the fumes of perfume.'

Dante couldn't imagine a more preposterous scenario if he tried, and nor could he understand the suddenly overwhelming urge to protect this woman from such circumstances that she would be willing to consider such an outrageous option—even if she was only joking. Those small, perfect hands of hers were not made for hard manual labour. No, he could think of much better uses to put those hands to, and none of them involved digging up concrete.

'You did not go to college or university?' he asked her, at a loss to know why she was doing a job she clearly disliked so much. A defensive look darkened her eyes and she crossed her arms in front of her chest as if subconsciously seeking protection from unhappy memories.

'No, I didn't. My family's circumstances weren't conducive to me going. I went out to work to support myself when I was sixteen.'

'You did not live at home?'

'Yes, I lived at home.' Swallowing down the almost intolerable ache inside her throat, Bliss made a snap decision to throw caution to the wind and tell this man the truth. It was a first for her. Hardly anyone knew the real circumstances of her family life, not even her best friend, Trudy. 'When I was sixteen, my mother took her own life. My father already had a drink problem and it simply got worse. I had to look after him as well as myself...then two years after Mum died he just walked out. All he left was a note telling me not to look for him. I haven't seen him in over seven years.'

Dante fell thoughtfully silent for a moment before speaking. 'That must have been…very difficult.'

Glancing up at him, her violet eyes flashing like little shards of coloured ice, Bliss shook her head.

'No. It was horrible and it was hell but it wasn't "difficult". Difficult means troublesome or perplexing and losing both my parents in the space of two years far exceeded that. Anyway…I don't know why I told you all that. I'm not generally known for spilling my guts to a complete stranger.'

CHAPTER FOUR

'I WOULD like to think by now that I am not a stranger to you, Bliss. And I am more sorry than I can say that such a terrible thing happened to you.'

Instinctively Dante understood what it must have cost her to reveal such personal heartbreak and he found the respect he already had for this surprising young woman steadily deepening, moment by moment.

'Well, we all have our cross to bear.' Rising to her feet, Bliss regarded Dante's undeniably impressive physique with a new wariness. Had she said too much? Would he question her reliability now that he knew she flitted from job to job and came from such an unsettled, tragic background? Feeling her spirits sink a little, Bliss knew she needed a diversion to prevent them from sinking even lower. A breath of fresh air before bed would be good—some time to regroup the defences that had undeniably come under attack as she'd been reminded of the sadness of her past. 'I'm popping out for a while. Shall I take a key so as not to disturb you?'

'There is no need.' Dante's glance was all-consuming and missed nothing. Certainly not her suddenly urgent desire to be alone to cope with the flood of sad memories. Straightening his shoulders as if to remind her of the innate gravitas in his bearing, he nodded very slightly, almost formally. 'I will wait up for you. While you are under my family's roof I am responsible for your care. But do not stay away long. It is neither right nor safe for a young woman to wander the city streets alone at night.'

Fiercely protective of her independence—simply because being independent was something that had become
a habit from a very young age—Bliss was about to snap
back at him that she didn't need looking after, but she
suddenly felt too weary. The fight just oozed out of her
like air from a punctured balloon, and she couldn't bring
herself to complain. Secretly, she also couldn't deny that
it was actually quite nice to have someone worrying
about her for a change.

'I won't be long,' she said softly, then quickly escaped
before her desire to stay within the safety and warmth of
this wonderful apartment with this equally wonderful
man became far too appealing to resist.

'I am taking you and my niece out to lunch today,' Dante
told her the next morning after breakfast. In the middle
of cleaning Renata's sticky face with a washcloth, Bliss
glanced at him across the table, everything inside her
tightening almost unbearably at the idea of going out in
public with this surprising man.

'You don't have to—'

'Tatiana is having a visit from a family friend—a priest
from my father's home in Varese. I am hoping he will
be able to offer her some much-needed consolation. So
we will wait until he comes, then we will go out. I have
already booked us a table.'

There was clearly no arguing with him this morning,
Bliss decided with resignation. His handsome face appeared strained and preoccupied, as if he was wrestling
with problems that were testing his patience and inge-
nuity to the maximum. She didn't doubt they were.
Tatiana still kept to her bed with no apparent sign of
wanting to move out of it. The doctor who had attended
her yesterday when Bliss had returned to her flat to get

her things had told Dante that he couldn't predict how long it would take his sister to recover from shock and grief. It was different with everybody, he said, although the phases the body and mind went through were the same. The family were clearly just going to have to bide their time and wait to see what happened.

Half an hour later, Tatiana's home help, a plump, smiling Italian woman named Sophia, arrived to see to the domestic chores that needed doing. As Bliss carried Renata back into the living room Dante followed her thoughtfully. 'You are feeling better today?' he wanted to know.

'Feeling better?' Frowning, Bliss pondered what he meant. Then she realised he was referring to her confession last night about her home life. Sensing her spine crawl with embarrassed heat, she put Renata down on the floor amongst her toys and glanced distractedly out of the window as if to gain some time to collect herself. 'Yes, I'm fine, thanks. Please don't think any more of what I said. It was late and I was tired.'

But it hadn't been *that* late, Dante recalled, and he guessed that the tiredness Bliss referred to had come more from enduring what she called her 'cross to bear' rather than physical fatigue.

'Mmm.' He wouldn't ignore her plea not to think any more about it…not right now. But he couldn't deny that, along with his primary concern for Tatiana and his niece, he had become intrigued with the young woman who had so readily come to the aid of his family. Later, perhaps, when Renata was in bed and they were alone, Dante would make a point of finding out some more of Bliss's story. Perhaps like him she had become too used to concealing her true self from those around her, particularly those who were close to her. Perhaps she needed to tell the truth to someone she didn't have a history with. Dante would wait and see. While he spent precious time with his sister and her little daughter—for the first time in a life that defined the word 'busy'—he would have plenty of time to reflect on his relationships. So why not include this latest one that had manifested with Bliss Maguire? After all…in his business he made a point of encouraging open and honest relationships with all his employees wherever he could…

'Who would have believed that twirling spaghetti round a fork could be as challenging as finding a water-hole in the Sahara?' Her features composed into a frustrated frown, Bliss glanced deliberately away as Dante focused his calm, measured gaze upon her across the table. With Renata seated in a high chair between them, her cute bow-shaped mouth liberally coated in tomato sauce, Dante knew that to the well-dressed onlookers in this up-market, bustling Italian restaurant owned by a family friend, the three of them must appear like a real family. *Mamma, papà, e bella bambina.* A possessive glint stole unknowingly into his eyes as he silently appraised the enchanting face of the pretty woman sitting opposite him. In her candy-pink blouse and smart black trousers, her make-up simple and understated, it was hard to notice any other woman in the room.

'Here. It is not so very difficult. Let me show you.'

But he didn't just show her. While Bliss stared in silent trepidation, like an awed observer watching a tightrope walker do impossible things on a high wire, he deftly wound some long spaghetti strands around his own fork and leant across the table to feed it into her startled mouth. With her heartbeat racing nineteen to the dozen, she tried to chew the delicious pasta with a modicum of grace, but the fact that Dante still sat, fork poised, staring at her with heat in his eyes, made the task almost impossible. Every emotion inside Bliss seemed to reach a crescendo of intensity, culminating in a silent yet desperate appeal to the heavens for help. It was a scary thing feeling so powerless to resist this man's undeniable charms and the roller-coaster sensation she experienced in the pit of her stomach every time Dante di Andrea glanced her way was becoming too much of an unsettling habit. As honourable as he undoubtedly was—clearly illustrated by the fact that he felt duty-bound to immediately step in and help his sister when she was in need—Bliss had no doubt in her mind that Dante was merely playing with her. Turning on that irresistible Latin charm just because he could. The biggest mistake she could make, Bliss decided, would be fooling herself into believing she was somehow special just because his heated gaze seemed to promise that, if she were in a line-up of beauty queens, it would be she he would choose above all else.

'I didn't know that eating spaghetti was such an art,' she quipped, patting her lips with her linen napkin, more to conceal her confusion than because it was strictly necessary.

'Neither did I,' Dante replied seriously. 'But you have made it one.'

'*Ciao*, my friend! It is good to see you…*è stato un molto tempo*.'

'Yes,' Dante agreed, rising briefly to his feet as an elegantly attired silver-haired man with smiling eyes enthusiastically captured his hand. 'It has been a long time, Raphael. Too long.'

'And this is your beautiful family? Why did I not know

that you had married and produced this charming little *bambina*?'

Before Dante or Bliss could say anything, Raphael bent down to a bemused Renata and kissed her soundly on both cheeks, apparently totally uncaring that he was in real danger of being covered in spaghetti sauce. The gesture was so unaffected and natural that Bliss found herself warming to the man. Glancing across the table at Dante, she wondered why his handsome face was set in a frown.

'Renata is my niece, Raphael. Bliss is a friend and I am still lamentably single.'

'What?' As Raphael straightened to his full height once more he cast a long appraising glance towards Bliss, then spoke to Dante in a flood of expressive Italian. When Dante merely smiled and shrugged in answer to this long, impassioned utterance, Raphael moved round the table to Bliss and soundly kissed her on both cheeks as well.

'*Bellissima!* You must not listen to my friend Dante when he tells you that you are just "friends". When I saw you just now, you both had eyes for nobody else but each other! It is clear to me that you must be together, no?'

Feeling her face suffuse with hot colour, Bliss didn't know what to say. Lifting her gaze to Dante's, she was shocked to find him apparently amused and in no immediate hurry to correct the completely wrong impression that his friend had gleaned of their situation. Why didn't he say something, for goodness sake?

'I am sorry, but you're wrong. I'm just…working for Mr di Andrea. That's all.'

Raphael clearly didn't accept this notion one little bit. Shaking his head and smiling at the same time, he regarded Bliss like a fond and doting *papà*. 'But you are perfect for each other. I, Raphael Destrieri, know this! You are beautiful and you are Italian, no?'

Unable to suppress a smile of her own, Bliss was genuinely regretful at having to deny yet another wrong assumption. 'No. I'm not Italian. My mother was English and my father Irish.'

Transfixed by the tiny dimple at the side of her mouth as she smiled at his friend, Dante sensed his interest deepening. She was half Irish? With a name like Maguire, he should have guessed. In discovering a similar connection to himself, Dante was strangely exhilarated. His father Antonio had told him many times that his mother had been bewitchingly beautiful. Dante had an old black-and-white photo his father had kept in his wallet, as proof. She too had been dark like Bliss, but, instead of ravishing violet eyes, his mother's eyes had been green, as green as the Emerald Isle she had come from.

'You have traced your family tree, no?' His lined brow puckering into a frown, Raphael pondered this new information as though working out a conundrum that intrigued him. Pausing to spoon a mouthful of food into Renny's mouth, Bliss shifted uncomfortably at the coil of deep unease that unravelled inside her at the mention of her family. *Here we go again,* she thought resignedly, pushing away the desolation that threatened. No matter how much or how often she told herself she'd come to terms with her troubled past and her own profound unhappiness at losing both her parents, she was still deeply affected by the turbulence of her years growing up with them.

'No. I haven't.'

'Then your *mamma* or *papà* have traced theirs? If not,

there must be some Italian blood somewhere. I know just by looking at you.'

'Raphael… Bliss is clearly not comfortable with your questioning, my friend. What does it matter where she is from? Perhaps we make too much of these things, huh?' It was not just Bliss who was ill at ease with Raphael's persistence in discovering her antecedents. Dante deliberately infused his voice with command.

'How can you say this? Of course where we come from is important! You and I are not family, but we are united by the common bond of our ancestors, no? Your father and my father came from the same small town in Italy. That counts for something, *sì*?'

'I did not say it was not important,' Dante said quietly, his own blood simmering with the complexity of feeling that the other man's words ignited inside him—feelings about belonging and identity that had plagued him all his thirty-three years. 'I am simply saying that other people may not be as passionate about it as you are.'

Having been made aware that the rest of the company was not warming to his subject as much as he was, Raphael sighed, threw his hands up in the air and smiled at its closure with easy and good-humoured acceptance. Turning to Bliss, he inclined his head slightly in a bow.

'Please forgive me if I have offended you, *mia cara*. I did not mean any harm by it.'

'You have not offended me at all, Signor Destrieri. Please think nothing of it,' Bliss quickly replied. When Renata held out her arms to be picked up, Bliss didn't think twice about lifting the little girl out of her high chair and into her arms. Diverted by the scene, both men fell into silence as they watched the child snuggle up against the fulsome curves beneath Bliss's candy-pink blouse and Bliss's fingers absently stroke her charge's soft silky hair as naturally as any devoted mother. Taken aback by the acute sense of longing that crowded his chest at the sight, Dante spoke to Raphael in his native tongue conveying to him that he and Bliss had things to discuss and promising to be in touch soon. They would meet for dinner or a drink together, Dante suggested, when he would gladly bring his friend up to date on all the family news. Placated by the suggestion, Raphael said a very charming goodbye to Bliss, fondly ruffled the little girl's hair, then firmly shook Dante's hand and heartily patted his back before leaving.

'What a nice man,' Bliss commented lightly, wondering at the same time at the slightly brooding expression that had stolen across Dante's face.

'He is a top connoisseur of art,' he told her, his gaze gravitating immediately towards her. 'And he recognises exceptional beauty when he sees it.'

Finding herself tongue-tied and overwhelmed by the meaning he so outrageously hinted at, Bliss dipped her eyes and softly kissed the top of Renata's head.

'Tatiana! What are you doing out of bed? Has Father Chinelli gone?'

The fragile-looking brunette dressed in a peach-coloured satin robe, her long hair curling around her shoulders, immediately rose to her feet from the couch she'd been curled up on, at their entrance. There was something about the expression in her sapphire eyes that made Bliss suddenly cling more tightly to Renata. The man to the side of her seemed to sense it too and his gaze briefly pulled away from his sister to touch her with a concerned, strangely possessive glance.

'Yes, Father Chinelli has gone. It was good to talk with him, Dante. Thank you for arranging it.'

'Your talk together must have made you feel better if you are up on your feet again, Ana.'

'It was not just Father Chinelli that has effected this change in me,' Tatiana replied, her generous mouth curving into an almost joyful smile. '*Mamma* has been on the phone to me, Dante. She has found *Papà* a wonderful nurse and is coming to stay with me tomorrow! What do you think about that?'

What did he think? For a moment Dante's thoughts were completely frozen. If his mother was coming tomorrow, then that would mean that they would no longer need Bliss's help with Renata. It would also mean that he would not have a reason to see her again. There was an almost painful emptiness inside him when he realised that—an emptiness that made no sense to him. How could it when he had known this woman barely any time at all? Yet he couldn't deny there was a connection between them—the atmosphere was as if the very air around them were holding its breath when they were together. And today in the restaurant at lunch—when he had fed her spaghetti and those bewitching violet eyes of hers had turned sultry and dark as they gazed back at him... *Mamma mia*! It had been all Dante could do to hold onto his reason! Desire for her had been swift and hot, like a Chinook wind in the Rocky Mountains where the temperature could increase dramatically in a matter of minutes. His friend Raphael's appearance had been timely to say the least...

'That is good news, Ana. When is she arriving? I will send a car to meet her at the airport.'

There was very little emotion in that deeply attractive voice of his, Bliss noticed with curiosity. Wasn't he pleased that his sister was clearly feeling so much better and that his mother was coming from Italy to help her?

Even if it did mean that Bliss's services would no longer be required. Her heart stalled at the thought, then picked up its beat again, like a train chugging its way out of the station. Today at the restaurant something very strange had happened. For the first time ever in her life she had fallen hard for a man. So hard that it left her feeling stunned and scared. But what was there to be scared about when after she left here she would probably never see him again? There would be no need. Except maybe Bliss's own heartfelt need to know that all was right in his world and that no harm had come to him.

Nothing could possibly come of her brief association with Dante di Andrea. He had his world and she had hers. And now both of them had to return to those worlds— the known and the familiar—and forget that they'd ever met…like strangers on a train whose gazes had briefly and passionately connected before they'd had to disembark at different stops.

'She will be arriving at three o'clock. Bliss, I am sorry that I will not need your help after tomorrow, but perhaps you will be kind enough to take care of Renata for me for one more night? I would like to take a bath and prepare things for my mother's visit. I would be most grateful for your help.'

'Of course. I am so glad you're feeling so much better, Tatiana.'

'*Grazie*. Oh, and Dante? *Mamma* says that there is some business problem back at the hotel in Milan. They need you back there, pronto.' Crossing the smooth maple wood floor to where Bliss stood with her daughter, Tatiana bestowed a warm kiss on her baby's cheek before returning to her bedroom and firmly closing the door.

Neither of the two remaining people in the room moved. For several moments the ensuing silence was so tangible that a blade could have cut straight through it. Then, slowly, Dante turned to study Bliss, a muscle throbbing slightly beneath the smooth surface of his tanned cheek, his emerald eyes narrowed as if he was having great trouble in maintaining a controlled façade.

'This is a surprise, no? I did not expect my mother to be able to arrange things for my father so soon. My sister is very close to her and you can see the difference in her already.'

'It's wonderful news, Dante. I'm sure having her mother here will help Tatiana enormously.'

'But you will go tomorrow? Back to your job at the store?'

What else could she do but agree? She was miserable at the very idea of going back to her job behind the beauty counter, but right now she didn't have an alternative. They had agreed to let her have a week's unpaid leave and so at least she would have a few days to herself to maybe think about finding other more suitable work before she had to go back. Thank heaven for small mercies. Raising her troubled gaze to his, Bliss adjusted Renata's weight more comfortably against her hip and forced her frozen lips into a reluctant smile.

'I have a few days before I absolutely have to go back so I'm going to make the most of them. My flat is long overdue for a tidy-up for a start, so I'll have plenty to do.'

'But you really do not want to go back?' Dante enquired softly.

Finding it almost impossible to meet his eyes, Bliss shrugged. 'There must be more to life than spraying expensive perfume on rich, pampered women who probably already have a bathroom full of the stuff! It's not exactly helping the world, is it?'

There was a glimmer of amusement amidst the tantalising green in Dante's gaze. 'And you like to help people…is that not so, Bliss?'

'Where I can, yes.'

'Then you are indeed wasted behind the beauty counter. Although I am certain you must help them sell a great many beauty products if the women who buy them aspire to look like you.'

'You must have gone to charm school from a baby! Compliments just roll off your tongue so easily.' Suddenly unable to keep the lid on the unhappiness that was seeping into her veins, Bliss turned away, wondering why she felt so hurt and angry. She knew the score. A gorgeous Italian male like Dante di Andrea thought nothing of dispensing such compliments to women, so why was she reacting so foolishly, as if he were stringing her along in some way? He'd only hired her to help his sister with her baby. Now that Tatiana was starting to make a recovery, it was obvious that Bliss wouldn't be needed any more. So what was there to feel cheated about?

'You do not think I mean what I say when I pay you a compliment?' He had taken hold of her arm, curling his big bronzed hand around her fragile, slender-boned wrist with something very close to angry possession. Bliss took a mental gulp.

'What does it matter? After tomorrow you'll never see me again anyway. I think Renny needs her afternoon nap. If you'll excuse me, I'll go and lay her down in her cot.'

'You may forget me, Bliss Maguire. But I will *not* forget you so easily.' Before Bliss could think another thought, Dante bent his dark head and claimed furious possession of her lips in an earth-stopping, demanding, bruising kiss that almost made her drop the child in her arms in shock.

CHAPTER FIVE

'YOU shouldn't have done that! Why did you?'

When he released her Bliss thought that her flow of breath might be affected for ever, such was the power and volcanic sensuality of Dante's kiss. There had been no warning that he might do such a thing and so she hadn't been a bit prepared to deal with it. Now she was on another planet spinning out of the cosmos because nothing made any earthly sense at all right then, save her deep craving for more of what Dante had to offer. Tingling and aching, her lips were already missing his devastating touch as if, in the instant they had become intimate, they had pledged themselves to him and only him. As Bliss's emotions swam with feelings and desires that crashed over her like hundred-foot waves her eyes bored into Dante's and saw that he too appeared deeply affected by what had just transpired between them. He was dragging his fingers agitatedly through the strong, silken strands of his deep black hair, and Bliss noticed his hand was ever so slightly shaking.

'You have to ask?' he ground out, his voice thick.

What could she say? Right now her feelings were in a torrent of confusion and Bliss hardly had an answer that made any sense. Her equilibrium had deserted her. She could still taste the silken glide of his tongue in her mouth and the impression lingered as though it were some carnal opiate, while his disturbing masculine scent was so imbued into her psyche that she knew she would never forget it. Oh, what had he done? Before Dante had kissed her, Bliss might—just might—have been able to walk away and preserve him as a pleasant, unexpected memory, but what was she supposed to do now?

Renata reached up and touched Bliss's cheek as if sensing something was amiss and for a moment Bliss willingly got lost in the wondrous radiance of those soft brown eyes.

'You obviously know something I don't,' she murmured.

Dante's harsh intake of breath amply illustrated a tension and anger she didn't understand. Wasn't she the one who should be mad at him? After all, Bliss would have to walk away and pretend that a landslide hadn't just occurred inside her. While for Dante, no doubt, she was just one more pretty face that he had briefly desired while they were together, but which would be just as swiftly forgotten when she left.

'I do not believe you do not know why I kissed you.' His mouth twisted slightly with derision and his arresting green eyes suggested the kind of Mediterranean heat that baked pavements in an instant. 'You are an intelligent woman and I do not believe that you cannot recognise desire when you see it.'

'I recognise it, Dante…but that doesn't mean I welcome it.'

Tearing her gaze away from his, Bliss folded Renata more securely in her arms and, fully aware that she was taking the coward's way out, quickly left the room before he could waylay her.

Her packing done, Bliss made another brief but thorough scan of the room she had occupied for just two short nights. Her melancholy gaze alighted on the yachts and cruisers that were anchored just outside the window—the sun glinting off their bright paintwork with prismatic brilliance, highlighting a world that was so vastly different from her own that comparisons were ludicrous. This was the élite stratosphere that Dante was a part of, she thought in a mixture of awe and resignation, suddenly struck anew by the contrast. A rare, moneyed sphere inhabited by wealthy entrepreneurs and inherited riches, where people were faced with the kind of choices Bliss could only dream about: which private island to holiday on in winter; what high-profile dress designer to monopolise this spring. And if his sister hadn't fainted in front of Bliss in the store that day, then her everyday, humdrum little life would not have been turned on its head so completely that she had no idea how to climb back on.

Now he was going to take her home on his way to the airport to pick up his mother, his mind no doubt focused on her arrival and his own imminent departure back to Italy. What had driven Dante to kiss her so intimately? He had taken possession of her lips as though he would die if he didn't, making heat scorch along her veins like a riptide. His touch had caused aftershocks so profound that Bliss asked herself if she'd ever really been awake in her life at all up until now. Such was the impact of the desire he had kindled into being.

'Bliss? Are you ready to go?'

From the other side of the door Dante's voice made every sense in her body clamour wildly for his attention and a soft, dismayed moan escaped her lips before she could prevent it. Then, securing the catch on her leather bag with trembling fingers, she briefly ran her fingers through her hair, took a final wistful glance at the seductive vision of the boats in the marina, then resolutely went to the door.

'I'm ready,' she said, her violet gaze deliberately averted as she swept past him into the corridor.

Carrying her bag up the two short flights of stairs, Dante wrinkled his nose a little with distaste at the sour, stale smell that lingered on the concrete landing along with the profound air of general neglect. He hadn't expected Bliss to live in the lap of luxury, but it disturbed him deeply that she lived in such a soulless place. She was like a pretty wild flower, he thought, growing amongst the cracks between concrete paving slabs: fragile yet hardy— lending beauty to a landscape that cried out for such relief. He had already deduced that her job probably did not pay very well, and obviously her accommodation choices were limited. But besides that, Dante knew that Bliss's heart was clearly not in her work at all. Knowing all of this, he had still been vaguely shocked by the stark contrast to his own extremely comfortable circumstances as they'd pulled up outside the run-down block of flats that Bliss had directed him to.

They'd argued over her means of getting home, Dante finally insisting that he drove her and Bliss reluctantly capitulating, clearly wanting to be rid of his presence as soon as possible so that she could resume her life without him. Only, Dante was nowhere near as sure as Bliss that he wanted to let her. The touch of her sweet lips against his had inflamed him as hotly and as fiercely as a lighted match to a pile of dry straw. It had stirred into life an ardour so great that he honestly didn't know what to do with all the pent-up energy and simmering need she had left him with. For such a long time he had become used to maintaining an almost detached attitude to the art of lovemaking—going through the motions but always keeping something of himself back. Now, however,

Dante was compelled to explore the possibilities that such a violent attraction presented. He would not be true to his passionate, hot-blooded nature if he didn't...

'Well, that's that, I suppose.'

Clearly not intending to invite him in, Bliss opened her front door and turned to regard him, her wary violet gaze hardly able to conceal the fact that she was upset. Did she regret leaving him and his adorable niece? For a long moment the thought prevented Dante from saying anything. Then warmth stole into his veins initiating feelings that wouldn't be tamped down—feelings that were currently taking over his body in a most disturbingly sensual and demanding way.

'I want to come in for a moment,' he said, pushing the door behind her wide. Bliss stared, her gaze transfixed by the disturbingly intense focus of his glittering green eyes and the growing heat she saw swirling in their depths.

'Why?'

Her voice was a husky rasp, and when Dante's big hand came to rest on her shoulder, squeezing it slightly before impelling her inside, Bliss hardly knew what to think. Closing the door and feeling a leap of pleasure inside him at the cosy, beautifully decorated hallway with its soft beige carpet and ecru-coloured walls that immediately evoked an atmosphere of calm, Dante expelled the tension-filled breath that had been trapped inside his chest. He realised that it was somehow important for him to know that Bliss had some beauty in her life. The outside of her home might leave much to be desired, but inside she had clearly created a soothing oasis that provided the necessary rest and relaxation for her troubled soul.

'I have to pay you.'

'P-pay me?' Somehow Bliss found herself backed up against the wall, her glance helplessly captured as she watched Dante deposit her bag on the carpet, then reach into his inside jacket pocket for a long cream vellum envelope. He held it out to her, a sexy hitch at the side of his beautiful mouth, a gesture that made Bliss's womb worryingly contract into a spasm that was almost painful. 'For coming to my sister's rescue and for being a good Samaritan.'

Bliss suddenly didn't want to take the money. It seemed wrong somehow. She'd only done what any self-respecting person would have done, hadn't she? To take payment for helping someone out when they were in a crisis just didn't sit well with the code of ethics that she lived by. Besides which, she had formed a frighteningly close attachment to little Renata over the past two days and was already missing the little girl too much. In fact, the thought of not having contact with her again had left her with an aching, empty space inside her that she didn't know how to fill.

'It's all right, Dante. I don't need payment. I was happy to help you and your sister. What happened to Tatiana was tragic. I certainly don't want to profit from it.'

'But we made an agreement, no?' His dark brows came together like a black thundercloud threatening a previously clement day, and Bliss curled her palms into fists at her side and fervently willed him to go so that she could breathe freely again. Had the hallway of her little flat always been this impossibly narrow? Or was it just the fact that having six feet plus of seriously gorgeous Italian male looming over her with mesmerising green eyes, holding her spellbound, was distorting her sense of perspective out of all proportion?

'You earned this money and I am grateful. Please take it. Tatiana will be offended if you don't.'

'No, Dante. My mind is made up. Tell Tatiana it was my privilege to help her and little Renny. Her daughter is delightful…just delightful.' Bliss was suddenly so choked up it was hard for her to speak. Betraying tears pooled in her eyes and in desperation she made to push away from the wall before Dante could transfix her any longer with the captivating power of his presence.

'You are crying…why?' Cornering her before she could move, he dropped the cream envelope onto the floor. Gently moving his fingers across the brow of her cheekbone to catch her tears, he regarded her gravely as though she was a complete enigma to him.

'I can't believe I'm acting like this! Please go, Dante, before I make a fool of myself completely.' She didn't want his kindness, or his comfort. Didn't he know it was too much for her to withstand? All Bliss wanted was for him to go. Only, her mind and her body were hardly in agreement about this decision. Not when the mere touch of his fingers across her tear-stained face could stir into being an ache that seemed to emanate from her very soul. The sheer power of that ache was consuming her whole body like a fire tearing through a house made of straw and if he didn't satiate it soon she might not be able to make sense ever again.

'I do not think you are foolish at all, Bliss. What you are is brave and beautiful…*bellissima*.'

'Don't say that! Don't pay me compliments I don't deserve.' She felt swamped by the evidence of passion she saw blazing in his eyes, and her mouth suddenly turned as arid as parched land that hadn't felt the kiss of rain for years.

'You cannot stop me from saying the truth. You will

only stop me if you kiss me and then I will quicken your blood with words that only spill from a lover's tongue, until you can be in no doubt that I am in earnest about my admiration for you.'

'No.'

'Yes, Bliss. *Sì.*'

When Dante's mouth created an explosive union with hers, the wall behind Bliss seemed to turn as liquid as her spine, her gasping, hungry breath melding with Dante's just before the heat and hardness of his demanding, sensuous lips made all thought impossible except for one ultimate realisation. The growing desire to surrender to the tearing wildness that was making her want to give herself to him, mind, body and soul. As her fingers latched on to the elegant hand-woven lapels of his tailored jacket as though the material were some kind of life-raft, Dante's own hands slid down her body to her waist, contact leaving an imprint so profound that Bliss began to shake. Bringing his hard, lean hips into full, dizzying proximity to hers, he passionately deepened the kiss. His tongue swept the tenderly silky depths of her mouth with stunning expertise designed to extract the ultimate response, almost unravelling her there and then before even a single item of her clothing was undone.

Dragging his lips from her mouth to her neck without breaking contact, he suckled her flesh, allowing his teeth to momentarily graze her skin before roughly tearing open Bliss's cotton shirt and consigning her buttons to oblivion. Too enraptured to want to protest, Bliss arched her body against him, desperate to feel the seductive satin of his hard, warm flesh against her own, mindless with longing. Murmuring something in his native tongue with a harsh, demanding breath, Dante ruthlessly gave the same tempestuous treatment to her bra, pushing aside the lace cups and releasing her pretty tip-tilted breasts into his big, smooth hands. Pinching her tight, swollen nipples until she bucked against him with a ragged cry, he took each one in turn into his mouth and introduced her to a nirvana so erotic that all Bliss could do was whimper and moan and bite her lip as wave after wave of powerful release throbbed through her body, leaving her as stunned as though she'd been buffeted by a hurricane.

'Where is your bedroom?' Raising his head, Dante stared down into Bliss's glazed violet eyes with possessive intent, his need to make her properly his urgent and primitive and driving every other coherent thought far from his mind. Trying to straighten her dishevelled clothing and meeting his avaricious gaze with equal hunger as she moved away from the wall, Bliss didn't reply— just headed dazedly down the hall to a door right at the end and went inside.

When Dante went through the door to join her, he had already removed his jacket and shoes and opened several buttons on his Italian-made shirt. At the edge of her bed, the dusky mulberry duvet already peeled back from damson-coloured pillows, Bliss was shakily taking off her own shirt and unbuttoning her jeans. As she stepped out of the heavy denim she deliberately didn't speak and neither did Dante. The very air that they shared said everything that needed to be said and more. It crackled around them, dense with anticipation and longing. She could have had her confidence stolen by her lack of experience in these matters, but, Bliss thought, why should she when Dante had already demonstrated his desire so openly? All she had to do was follow his lead and she would know what to do. If she faltered, or felt suddenly shy—then Dante would no doubt be a willing guide.

He removed his shirt and Bliss's gaze was magnetised

by the awesome beauty of his body. His chest was wide and bronzed, well defined and clearly toned to mouth-watering perfection beneath the swirls of fine dark hair that dusted across his flat male nipples. One corner of his mouth edged up in a lustful little smile as he came towards her and Bliss shivered violently. In one fluid motion he stepped out of the rest of his clothing, then, without breaking his gaze from hers, joined Bliss at the side of the bed, his mouth hotly touching her bare shoulder, then his hands slowly but surely pushing her back down against the pillows.

The panties she was wearing were a high-legged black confection of silk and lace fastened by little pink bows at the side and she had the body to exhibit them to their sexiest advantage. Allowing his glance to linger on the curvaceous flare of her hips to the tops of her shapely toned thighs, Dante sensed the need in him grow into a conflagration. Undoing the tiny hooks of her matching black bra with a sleight of hand that made Bliss almost forget to breathe, he feasted his appreciative male gaze on the gorgeous, erotic swell of breasts that would make an artist weep at the sight of such perfection. Everything about Bliss Maguire was as tempting as sin, Dante thought fervently, yet she had a delightful innocence that could not be fabricated. Excitement and ardour made his heart beat almost dangerously fast. With a sensuous rasp in Bliss's ear, describing to her in explicit Italian exactly what he'd like to do to her, he helped her part company with her sexy black underwear before she could beg him to tell her in English. Running his hand up the inside of her thigh, he found the clutch of tight curls at her apex, then eased his fingers slowly but inexorably into the damp warmth between her thighs. She whimpered—the soft, impossibly sexy sounds she was making heightening

his desire into a lightning storm in response. He sensed
the bounds of self-restraint snap and, uttering words that
sounded like an impassioned prayer, his mouth eagerly
sought hers in a highly charged, erotic kiss.

Unable to wait any longer he eased his throbbing, aching sex inside her, feeling himself harden to a degree that
was nothing less than exquisite torture at the deeply sensual contact. Lust deluging him in its power, like powerful water rapids urging him inevitably onwards to the
crest of a fall, he registered the hot clasp of Bliss's tight,
contracting muscles close around him in deeply carnal
feminine possession. As he kissed her everywhere the
taste and texture of her skin all but drove him close to
losing his sanity. But wherever and however much he
touched her, he found he was still greedy for more—like
a man who had been starved of sustenance for too long
and now could hardly contain his appetite.

The pleasure that consumed her was so amazing that
Bliss could hardly bear it. On some deeply unconscious
level she wondered if all this time she had somehow,
some way, been searching for this man all her life. As
he took hungry possession of her body time after time,
his hot Italian gaze melting her to her very bones, her
mind raced with how she was ever going to settle for
everyday reality ever again. The man was so extraordinarily beautiful—like a dream she hadn't known she'd
ached for until she'd experienced it in all its breathtaking
glory. Next to him all of the world's jewels would appear
lacklustre. It was hard for Bliss to believe that he could
want her with such dazzling ardour when he could surely
make love to any woman in the world besides her. Her
femininity soared with a power that was exhilarating. In
his arms she felt equally beautiful. Wanted and desired
beyond reason. To hope for more than this was surely

some kind of sin. Dante's loving had transported her to a heaven previously undreamed of and how many women could claim to have experienced the same?

Knowing she was close to release, Bliss willingly rocked her hips in time with the increasingly demanding rhythm of Dante's body. Her violet eyes turned dark as a black velvet sea as desire crested to a peak and crashed over her like a giant waterfall dragging her under, until all she could do was simply yield to nature's awesome power. But, before the erratic cadence of her heartbeat could return to anywhere near normal, Dante too found the completion he had been hungrily intent on, lowering himself against her body in a flood of passionate Italian, his scalding seed spilling into her like liquid flame. In the aftermath, Bliss hardly dared breathe in case she disturbed the intense feeling of satisfaction and joy that washed over her at accepting his loving into her body.

As he rolled over to lay by her side, Dante's sensuously formed lips eased upwards in a purely male smile of profound satisfaction. It was the smile of a man who had emphatically left his mark on the woman he had chosen and made no apology for doing so.

Bliss was momentarily transfixed by the gesture. Then her heart almost jumped out of her chest when she suddenly fully realised what they had just done.

'Dante! We—you didn't use anything! I'm not even on the pill!'

'*Maledizione!*' He turned abruptly at her panicked words, a cloud casting itself across his perfectly aligned features. He shook his head. 'Forgive me, *innamorata*. I should not have left such things to chance, but I was unprepared myself for what has just happened. *Sono idiota!* I can assure you there is no other risk, but—you will of course be alert to consequences? Do you want me to assist you, take you to a doctor to be sure?'

Bliss scooted up onto her elbow. A mixture of awe and wonder quickly replaced the concern that had been building on her face as she glanced down at him. Unable to resist the magnetic pull of his strong resolute jaw, her fingers traced the powerfully compelling outline of those passionately seductive lips of his, like a sculptor wondering how she could transfer such sublime perfection to cold, inanimate marble.

'I'm sure I'll be all right. It's a safe time,' she murmured, not wanting to spoil the wonder of their time together with worry about what might or might not happen in the future. 'Dante,' she breathed softly, her gaze drifting across his handsome, indomitable features with open admiration. His big hand captured hers and brought it slowly and sensuously to his lips, where he kissed her flesh with almost reverent adoration.

'Do you know what you have done to me?' he asked with a smile that hurt Bliss's heart. 'You have given me almost too much pleasure. The kind of pleasure that, once tasted, a man could never forget.'

Could she believe him? Bliss tortured herself jealously, imagining all the other women he must have made love to in the past. Was it only the fact that his body was replete with lovemaking that he paid her such a fulsome compliment? Her only other lover besides Dante had been an eighteen-year-old schoolboy she had had a crush on when she was just sixteen. He had been the most fancied boy in her school and Bliss had been shocked to her bones when she had found out that he had reciprocated her crush with equal ardour. He had even cried when she had told him she wouldn't see him again after he had helped her lose her virginity. But then he hadn't known that Bliss had just lost her mother and the only reason she had given herself to him so freely was so that she could feel something other than the horrible sensation of being trapped inside a block of ice for the rest of eternity.

'You almost make me want to believe that's true.' Her mouth curving into a softly wistful smile, Bliss rested her hand on the hard, ridged muscles of Dante's awesome bronzed chest with profound regret. 'But we probably won't see each other again after this, will we? You'll go back to Italy, back to your busy life, and you'll forget all about me.'

'Why do you think that?' Sliding up into a sitting position and fixing a plump damson pillow strategically behind his back, Dante slid his hand down Bliss's bare arm, secretly delighting in the display of goose-pimples that his touch made appear. As he stared into her worried face, once again feeling the beginnings of desire stirring in his loins as he enjoyed the stunning beauty of her clear violet gaze, Dante's glance was both possessive and unflinching. 'You think I can forget what we have between us so easily, as if it means nothing to me?'

'Even if it does mean something to you, we both know it won't lead anywhere.' Bliss's voice was steady and certain and was highlighted by the determined set of her small, perfect jaw. 'We have to be realistic. You have to go back home and I need to focus on finding a better job that will pay me a good enough wage to keep the roof over my head. I didn't expect this to happen. But now that it has…' She tucked her hair behind her ears and leant back against another pillow, sighing heavily. 'What I'm trying to say is that you don't have to worry. I'm not looking for a relationship and neither are you, so I can accept the fact we won't see each other again.'

Did she mean that? Dante wondered with a little frisson of shock and anger running down his spine. Was she really willing to dismiss their passionate interlude so readily? Such an idea was anathema to him. It wounded his pride as well as his already vulnerable heart. But he was not willing to expose such weaknesses to the woman by his side—no matter how passionately he desired her. And she was in for a surprise if she thought that he would just walk away without looking back, as if he had neither honour nor principles. He had made love to her. That was not something Dante took lightly. Especially not when he had experienced a connection with this woman that went deep beyond physical attraction. 'No, *innamorata*. I do not accept we cannot see each other again because of such inconsequential considerations. I may have to go home to Italy, but I will be back. We can meet and have dinner, and what is to prevent us from merely enjoying each other's company from time to time when I am here?'

His emerald eyes lightly skimmed her features, finally alighting with pleasure on her slightly parted, moistened lips, his emphasis on the word 'enjoying' leaving Bliss in no doubt as to exactly what that meant. Her skin throbbed with heat as she tried to also understand how Dante could dismiss the glaring difficulty of them possibly having a relationship when they were living in totally different countries and experiencing completely different lifestyles.

'You really want to see me again?' she asked in a quiet voice. 'Because I don't think it's a good—'

Dante bent his head and claimed her lips once more in a hard, demonstrative kiss that made her shiver. 'I want to see you again, and I will. Make no mistake about that. But now I have to go. I have some urgent problems to attend to, as you know. Forgive me, *dolcezza*. But I promise you we shall see each other again soon.'

Her skin feeling chilled where he removed the warmth of his body from hers, disappointment making her heart ache, Bliss watched him collect his clothes from the end of the bed where he had discarded them and step out onto the carpet to get dressed.

She told herself she should be relieved that Dante didn't act like a stereotypical playboy when clearly he had all the assets to do just that, but she still found it hard to believe that he really meant to see her again. And saying he wanted to see her again was one thing; actually following through on his intention once he'd returned to his wealthy lifestyle in Italy was another. She should just endeavour to behave like any other sophisticated woman of the world and simply let him go without any expectations. Even if it hurt like hell to do so.

'Bliss?' Pausing as he did up the zip on his trousers and pulled on his shirt, Dante examined her in the bed, her softly mussed hair and bare shoulders filling him with an almost impossible urge to join her again and seduce her once more before he left.

'I will repeat what I have just said. I am coming back to see you just as soon as I can.'

Pursing her lips, Bliss nodded, dragging the bedcovers more securely up to her chest. Whether she could believe what he said or not, she would hold on to the tiny hope that Dante *would* keep his word. She was helplessly distracted by his indomitable male beauty that made her small, plain bedroom seem far too inadequate a setting for such a magnificent jewel; his promise had the unsettling effect of making her feel somehow protected. Shocked to realise it, Bliss determinedly shook off the sensation of warmth that had stealthily crept into her limbs at his words. Was she building herself up for a big fall, hoping against hope that he might come back?

'Dante?'

'What is it?' His heated gaze honed in on her small heart-shaped face and those ravishing black-lashed violet eyes. Never before with a woman had he been in such turmoil about whether to stay or leave.

'Give Renny a kiss for me when you see her, won't you?'

Briefly absorbing the swift stab of pain inside his chest that her words elicited, Dante nodded curtly. '*Sì*. No problem.' And with that, he turned abruptly and left.

CHAPTER SIX

FINDING herself unexpectedly in a lull as customer demand in the store eased towards the end of the afternoon, Bliss took a moment to examine her overly bright eyes and pinked cheeks in the oval make-up mirror on the counter. She hadn't had the best start to the day. She'd woken feeling hot and shivery with a sore throat, but had convinced herself to ignore the feelings and just get ready for work. Now at nearly five in the afternoon she was feeling even hotter, the ache in her throat was akin to the pain of swallowing stinging nettles and she could no longer deny that she was obviously coming down with a cold. She prayed it was nothing more than that, because next week she would start her new job as a receptionist in a recently opened alternative therapy centre near where she lived and for once she was looking forward to the prospect of changing jobs. At least she would be working in an environment that was helping people, she'd told herself when she'd come away from the interview. The surroundings were bright and pleasant, and soothing ambient music was piped from unseen speakers throughout the day to calm frayed nerves and imbue customers with a sense of peace after the stresses of the outside world. It might not be enough to launch her into the career of the century, but at least she would be doing something useful. Surprisingly, the pay wasn't bad either.

Just before she turned away from the mirror, Bliss experienced the most acute tingling bordering on pain in her breasts. The sensation took her by surprise and she saw the alarm that registered in the darkened pupils of her vividly coloured eyes reflected back at her. Her hand went almost inadvertently to her trim, flat stomach beneath her fitted black skirt and about the same time she sensed her womb contract. Seeking the high chrome stool behind her that they used for customers who wanted make-up advice, Bliss eased her way onto it almost in a daze, her heartbeat thundering inside her chest. A realisation was surfacing somewhere in her brain yet again— a realisation that she'd been trying desperately to push away for some time now in the hope that she wouldn't have to face it.

Almost six weeks ago to the day, she had succumbed to the temptation of Dante di Andrea and allowed herself to be caught up in a tide of passion so profound that every inch of skin on her body was bathed in heat every time she recalled it. Despite his impassioned vow that he wanted to see her again, he had been conspicuous by his absence. Not that Bliss had really believed that he would come back. He was probably still in Italy, far too absorbed in his work to even remember the woman he had bedded so passionately one fine spring morning in London. Tears stung her eyes, angry, confounded tears because she had acted so foolishly and so thoughtlessly without a mind to what could happen. They definitely *weren't* tears of regret or sorrow that the man she had given herself to with such unthinking fervour had apparently deserted her, despite his promise. She'd never wanted the commitment of a relationship, so why did her stomach turn over at the thought of not ever seeing Dante again? The handsome Italian had got to her badly with his devouring emerald gaze and spine-tingling attention and there was apparently nothing Bliss could do about it, no matter how much she might protest that she wasn't looking for a relationship.

But… *Oh, Lord, I can't be pregnant!* Groaning beneath her breath, Bliss shut her eyes to absorb the waves of shock and distress that were washing over her. Placing her hand on her already feverish forehead, she sighed deeply. She wasn't usually a 'bury your head in the sand' type of person, but somehow she had found herself acting exactly that way. She had convinced herself that they'd slipped up at a safe time, and so she hadn't taken the morning-after pill. She'd had signs that she might be pregnant since missing her period, but she had somehow subconsciously clung to the idea that she *wasn't*. Now it was time to face the truth.

'What's up, gorgeous?'

She opened her eyes to find Trudy standing there, her pretty face frowning back at her with concerned curiosity. 'Not feeling well?'

'Can we go for a coffee after work?' Bliss suggested, knowing there was nothing for it but to share her fear about the possibility of her being pregnant with her closest friend. Right now, even though she'd like nothing better than to crawl into bed and sleep for the next three days, Bliss knew she couldn't keep her secret anxiety to herself without driving herself crazy. Trudy was always good to talk to and often came up with the best advice.

'I'll meet you out front in half an hour,' Trudy agreed without a murmur, the other girl realising instinctively that this must be something serious.

'So basically it's decision time, isn't it?' Taking a sip of frothy coffee, Trudy focused her steady blue gaze on the dark-haired girl sitting opposite. Bliss hadn't touched her coffee, finding herself suddenly nauseous at even the thought of drinking it. She sat in the half-empty coffee house staring down at the polished wooden table, first absently fingering the sugar bowl, then turning her un-opened caramelised biscuit over and over in her hands, her thoughts as jumpy and ephemeral as a butterfly.

'Decision time?' she repeated, her thoughts finally focusing.

'The baby. Bliss, you've hardly been listening to one word I've said!'

'Yes, I have…'

'You're going to have to decide, and soon. You're starting a new job on Monday, what are you going to tell them?'

'Let's not panic, right? I don't even know if I am pregnant yet until I do a test.' But even to her own ears her sensible-sounding statement lacked even an ounce of conviction. *She was pregnant with Dante's baby.* She could deny it to herself until the sun stopped rising in the sky, but that would be irresponsible and juvenile, and Bliss prided herself on being neither of those things.

'I'm not having a termination.' There; she'd said it. She'd voiced the one solid realisation that had come to her in the last half hour. Bliss didn't doubt bringing up a baby on her own as a single mother was going to be her biggest challenge to date, but even harder was the idea of a termination. This was *her* child, a precious life that was growing inside her. The thought made her heart leap.

'Why did I know you were going to say that?' Catching her hand in her own, Trudy reached out to Bliss as the true friend she was, instantly understanding the decision her best friend had made without judging it one way or the other. 'It's going to be hard, you know that? And what about the father? This Daniel di—'

'Dante.' Unable to prevent herself from colouring at the easily familiar way she pronounced his name, Bliss finally took a sip of her coffee and instantly felt sick. 'Excuse me. I've got to go to the bathroom.' Unceremoniously scraping back her chair, she hurried towards the ladies' toilets, leaving Trudy staring after her with concern as she went.

Not finding Bliss at home, Dante drove round the block several times to gather his thoughts, contemplating where she could be and speculating at what time he could expect her to return. He refused to believe she was away, or wouldn't be returning home that evening. He was far too impatient to see her for that. All the way on the drive over from the di Andrea hotel in Belgravia he had wrestled with what he was going to say to her, since there had been no communication between them for six long weeks. Already he'd realised that she would not be impressed with the excuse that he'd been heavily involved in important negotiations back home to acquire two new hotels, one in St Tropez, and the other in Lake Como. The one in Lake Como he and his father planned to make as a gift to Tatiana. Antonio di Andrea, ill as he was, wanted his 'baby girl' and his youngest grandchild to come home again and this was the way he proposed to persuade her. Before she'd gone to the UK, Tatiana too had worked with the family in the hotel business. Then she'd gone to England to study, where she'd met and fallen in love with Matt Ward. Now Antonio had been diagnosed with a serious heart complaint and he fretted he would not live to see his darling Renata grown. Dante had promised to help persuade Tatiana to see the sense in returning home to Italy. Lake Como was beautiful and helping to run the hotel would, in time, assist her in coming to terms with her terrible loss.

Having had most of his time back in Italy monopolised by Antonio's eager plans for his daughter's future, Dante had hardly had a moment to think about Bliss Maguire and that incredible morning that he'd made love to her. But think about her he had, in the still of the night, in his big king-sized bed with the imported silk sheets from Saudi Arabia. His mind and body drowned in intoxicated heat at just the thought of having her there with him, helping to obliterate the stresses and strains of his working day with her soft, breathless sighs and a body whose lovely lines his hands would recognise even if he were blind.

Parking the dark blue Mercedes in a dominant position in the concrete car park where it would be in full view, Dante silenced the engine, then glanced once again at the time on his solid gold watch. It was almost eight thirty in the evening and there was still no sign of Bliss. He gave vent to his frustration in his own tongue as he glared into the side-view mirror, then sat bolt upright as a black taxi pulled up beside him and Bliss stepped out. She was wearing a pink linen jacket over her slim black skirt and Dante noticed immediately that she'd cut her hair. It had been shaped to frame her lovely heart-shaped face and, even in the fading evening light, Dante could see the glossy shine on it. Smiling at something the driver said as she handed over the fare, she moved aside with a short wave as he drove off again. Dante immediately got out of the car and slammed the door.

'You are home late,' he said out loud in his accented English. He saw her turn round in surprise and shock, her skin turning pale at the sight of him.

'Dante. What are *you* doing here?'

'I told you I would be back. Clearly you did not believe me.'

'That was six weeks ago! Can you blame me?'

'When I make a promise, I keep it. I would have been in touch sooner, but the demands of my work prevented me.' Dante's voice was grave and he clearly did not like the idea that she had doubted his word.

'How are you? How is Tatiana, and little Renata?' Telling herself to keep the conversation light and not let him see how totally shocked she was to see him, Bliss knew it was a tall order when inside her all her senses were reacting as though she'd just bungee jumped into the Grand Canyon. He looked so gorgeous and self-possessed as he stood there; so out of place in this cold, concrete, graffiti-smeared car park—as incongruous as a royal prince turning up in a dole queue. Bliss hadn't forgotten how handsome his features were, how resolute and sculpted his jaw or how riveting his eyes—yet seeing him again in the flesh, dressed to kill in another exquisitely tailored suit, was almost too much for her already beleaguered senses to bear.

'Tatiana is well. Renata is growing fast and keeping her mother busy.'

'I'm very relieved. I was worried about them,' Bliss confessed.

'Then I am glad that I can put your mind at rest. Shall we go inside?'

'Inside?' With her door key held firmly in her closed palm, Bliss swallowed over the painful rawness in her throat. Her head was swimming as though it had been shaken up like one of those snow globes, and she was certain her temperature had just gone up a degree on seeing Dante standing there. Now it seemed her legs had turned to liquid rubber at the very idea of inviting this man over her threshold once again. Especially when she recalled what had happened the last time…

'It's getting late and I'm very tired. Why don't we make it another night instead?' she suggested hopefully.

'No. Now is good. Give me your bag—I will carry it upstairs for you.'

'I can manage.' She didn't welcome the autocratic tone in his voice. She was feeling too raw inside to be told what to do by anyone. She had bought a pregnancy test on the way home, gone back to Trudy's to use it and had her already strong suspicions confirmed. To find Dante waiting for her in the car park of the flats where she lived, on the very day she'd discovered it was irrefutable fact that she was having his baby, was the kind of timing you couldn't plan. Now all she needed was to discover she didn't have a job to go on Monday and that would be the icing on the cake. Weariness washed over her like enervating steam from a Turkish bath.

Dante saw her shoulders droop and her face become even paler. Instantly concerned at the tired picture that she presented, he went to her side, retrieved her heavy leather shoulder bag and, with his hand behind the small of her back, guided her up the concrete staircase to her flat.

'Why do you look so tired? What have you been doing with yourself?' When she struggled to fit her key inside the lock, Dante took that too and did the honours. Inside the small hallway he put down her bag and shut the door behind them. Then he turned back to Bliss to examine her properly, the cadence of his heart increasing almost dramatically at the sight of her. 'And why did you cut your beautiful hair?'

'Oh, for goodness' sake!' Her tone exasperated, Bliss

dragged her fingers through her shortened hair and grimaced at the gorgeous hunk of male towering over her.

'So many questions. My head is spinning!' It wasn't a
lie either. If she didn't sit down soon, she'd fall down.
Pushing open a door, she went into her recently tidied
living room and flopped down onto the cushion-laden
couch. Dante followed, his tanned brow furrowed as if
her behaviour was severely taxing his patience.

'You do not look well.' Recognising that beneath the
pallor of her skin there was a definite hint of a flush—
the kind a person acquired when they were running a
temperature—Dante's initial concern was swiftly renewed. 'Why did you go into work today if you were not
well?' He knew he was bombarding her with his questions, but he couldn't help it. It alarmed him immensely
to think that she had no one else to voice concern over
her well-being, especially since she had come so willingly and unquestioningly to Tatiana's aid in the store
that day, then again when she'd stayed to help with little
Renata.

'Because I have to earn my living, that's why!' She
hadn't meant to shout, but in a way anger helped Bliss
to hold back the more powerful underlying emotion that
was threatening to engulf her. A need for Dante to hold
her, to cradle her against that comforting, hard-muscled
chest of his, was growing inside her at such a rate as to
scare her witless. What was she thinking of? Did she
imagine for one second that he would welcome such a
display of feminine weakness? He'd probably run a mile
if he thought she needed him in any way, let alone if he
found out she was pregnant with his baby! But he mustn't
find out. Bliss was determined on that score. He was
obviously in London visiting his sister and maybe he'd
even thought to experience a repeat performance of what

had happened between him and Bliss the last time they'd been together in her flat, but casual sex could not and would not be on the agenda. No matter how powerful her attraction for him.

'Have you eaten?' Sighing, Dante dropped down onto the couch beside her, his hands linked together across his powerful thighs in his designer suit.

'I'm not hungry. When did you get back from Italy?'

'Yesterday. I've been staying in Belgravia.'

'At your family's hotel?' Bliss stole a greedy glance at his flawless chiselled profile.

'Yes.'

One small word, Bliss thought desperately, and it could make her melt as if her very bones were fashioned out of candle wax.

'It is clear to me that you have been working too hard, Bliss. What you need is a holiday. Why don't you come back to Italy with me?'

His suggestion was so surprising and so completely unexpected that Bliss experienced a wave of dizziness. The feeling was so disorienting that immediately she felt nauseous—just as she had done in the coffee house with Trudy. Terrified she was going to disgrace herself in front of him, she covered her mouth with her hand and made a dash across the room and out of the door to the bathroom.

'Bliss? Bliss, are you all right?'

He rapped hard on the locked bathroom door, fresh concern adding a commanding edge to his voice. 'Open the door immediately! What is wrong? Tell me!'

After a few seconds Bliss opened the door, her face white. Her beautiful violet eyes were wary and glazed with unshed tears. Dante stared. 'Do you need a doctor?'

he demanded, pushing away the surge of fear that rose up inside him.

'No. I don't need a doctor. I think I'm coming down with a cold, that's all.' She pushed past him, wondering desperately what she could say to make him go, because if he stayed around much longer she was afraid she might just break down and make a fool of herself. It went against the grain to feel so vulnerable and weak. Weakness or vulnerability had no place in her life. Bliss had understood from a very young age that inner strength was vital if she was going to survive in the world—doubly so, given her family's history.

'I just need to rest,' she told him when he followed her back into the living room. 'Perhaps you'd better go.'

'You did not answer me when I suggested you should come back to Italy with me for a holiday,' Dante replied firmly, his face hardening.

'Why, Dante? Because you think you owe me something because of what happened between us? Then let me reassure you that you don't. You can leave with a clear conscience as far as I'm concerned.'

'And you also did not cash the cheque I left you.' His gaze glittering with fury, he irritably pushed a lock of sable hair away from his brow. 'I paid you for helping my sister and you insult me by not accepting that payment. Now you insult me further by suggesting I am offering you a holiday because we made love and I feel guilty! *Il mio Dio!*'

'I don't want to argue with you.' Wishing she didn't feel so weak and under the weather, Bliss dropped back down again onto the couch. She still hadn't taken off her jacket because right now she welcomed the extra warmth it gave her.

'And I don't mean to insult you…no matter what you think.'

He could see that she was obviously tired. Biting back the frustration that was knotting every muscle in his body with profound tension, Dante decided to take charge of the situation.

'Well, we will talk about that tomorrow. What I think you should do right now is go straight to bed. If you are not feeling better in the morning I will phone for a doctor. I will stay here tonight and make sure you do not get any worse.' He loosened his expensive silk tie, rubbed a hand around the back of his collar and regarded Bliss as though he expected her to take action immediately. Dumbfounded, she stared up at his tall, commanding figure and felt her stomach execute a neat somersault.

'You're not serious?'

'Why not?' His green-eyed gaze narrowing with suspicion, Dante frowned.

'I don't want you to stay! If you're staying because of some misguided sense of loyalty where I'm concerned, then I release you from any such ridiculous obligation. I'm quite capable of taking care of myself. I don't need your help.'

'It is clear to me that you do.'

Removing his jacket, a fine specimen of exquisitely perfect tailoring that only the seriously rich and those with immaculate taste could afford to indulge in, he folded it casually across the back of a chair and stood, arms crossed. Meanwhile, his eyes tracked her every move as though he half expected her to make a run for it.

'I want you to go, Dante! I don't want you to stay here!' Desperately raising her agitated gaze to his, Bliss begged for his understanding. The last thing in the world she wanted him to do was stay the night and bear witness to her increasingly growing lack of control over the contents of her stomach—all because she was pregnant...

'Then, on this occasion, *innamorata*, I am overriding such desire. You helped my sister in her hour of need and now it is my turn to help you. Your couch looks extremely comfortable. I will spend the night there.'

Bliss once again sensed the colour leach from her face. As Dante firmly planted his feet in front of the door she jumped up, pushed him aside and fled once more to the bathroom, feeling more wretched and afraid than she'd felt since her mother had taken her own life.

CHAPTER SEVEN

RAISING the pastel-green curtain to view a drizzly, un-inspiring dawn, Bliss sighed heavily, dropped the curtain back into place, then walked heavy-footed back to her bed. The tossed duvet and pillows looked as if she'd had a fight with them and clearly illustrated that she'd hardly slept a wink. Now she was feeling as flat as a sofa cushion that had lost all its stuffing, weary to the bone and queasy. There was no way she'd be able to go in to work today. Perching on the edge of the bed, she tried desperately hard to control the need to rush straight to the bathroom again. It didn't help her sense of losing control that Dante had probably spent an equally restless night on her couch, his tall, muscular frame clearly far too big to be remotely comfortable on a piece of furniture that was hardly the height of luxury and ease. Why had he insisted on doing such a crazy, unexpected thing? He'd been adamant he was going to stay even in the face of her disagreement, but this morning she wanted to make it clear to him that she didn't need a minder—now or ever. Besides…she had to get him out of the house before there was the remotest chance he would find out about her condition.

Searching through kitchen cupboards, Dante found some coffee grounds, a small cafetière and two mugs. As he stood waiting for the kettle to come to the boil he stretched his arms wide, then rolled his head from side to side to ease out the kinks in his neck. He had not enjoyed the best night's rest known to man on Bliss's couch and this morning his body felt as though it had been locked inside a hamster cage, such was the stiffness in his limbs. But he wasn't complaining, because at least he had had the satisfaction of being close to Bliss.

When he had peered into her room a couple of times to check on her, it had been to find that she'd kicked all her bedclothes aside, but he'd hesitated in covering her up because she was clearly a little feverish. Her skin had had the blush-pink sheen to it that people often had when they were running a temperature. Biting back his anxiety as well as the urge to let his gaze linger on the smooth, taut limbs revealed by her lack of covers, all Dante had been able to do was pray that by the morning her temperature would be back to normal again. If it wasn't he would be calling upon a doctor friend of the family who worked in Harley Street, for advice. Sandrine Lantain had been a GP before she'd decided to specialise and Dante knew she wouldn't mind seeing Bliss at short notice if he asked her to.

In his opinion what Bliss needed most was a holiday and today he planned on persuading her to come back to Italy with him. If she told him she could not due to work commitments, then Dante fully intended to find her another, better job on her return; one where the holiday entitlement was good and where she would definitely have the prospect of advancing her career if she so wished. He'd even toyed with the idea of finding her work in Italy—that way he could keep an even closer eye on her and maybe persuade her that they should see each other on a regular basis. The idea had been growing in him ever since he had left her that morning after they had made love. *Made love*...somehow the description didn't seem enough to describe the wild torrent of emotion that had erupted between them so hotly. Dante had a passionate nature, but it had not been his fortune to experience such an explosive intensity of emotion or earth-shattering pleasure with any other woman before. With Bliss, every emotion and desire he possessed was exquisitely heightened so that even just thinking of her he felt heat start to rise in his body.

'You've found the coffee, I see.'

She was suddenly framed in the kitchen doorway, her dark hair becomingly tousled, her body robed in a thin, silky coral-pink wrap that barely reached her knees. And such knees, Dante thought with satisfaction, his enthusiasm growing on the subject. Her legs were also shapely and elegant, with beautiful feet that arched prettily with perfectly trimmed pink toenails. His glance slid back slowly to her face and, to his utmost pleasure, he discovered that his openly appreciative admiration of her bare legs had caused her to colour delightfully.

'You have discovered my one vice. Without coffee in the morning I am—what do you say? A bear with a bad head?'

Her heart thudding at the laughter in his stunning green eyes, Bliss clutched at the front of her robe and slowly let out her breath. She didn't know about 'bear with a bad head'; 'most stunning male in the universe' was the epithet that most readily sprang to mind.

'Sore head. It's *sore* head, not *bad*.'

He shrugged as if the distinction was of no consequence. Which of course it wasn't.

'You want some?' he asked her, the laughter in his eyes dying away to be replaced by a much more intense look that made Bliss hot and shivery all at once.

'Some coffee, you mean?' She quickly shook her head. Already the potent smell of the coffee grounds in the opened jar was making her poor stomach heave. 'No thanks. I don't want anything this morning.'

'You are still feeling unwell?'

Her sore throat had eased a little and her temperature too, but, yes, she wasn't exactly feeling on top of the world, Bliss silently acknowledged. In fact, if she didn't get to the bathroom pronto, she would soon illustrate to the gorgeous male specimen standing in her kitchen that she was feeling anything *but* well.

'Bliss!'

This time Dante was too quick for her, reaching the bathroom door at exactly the same time as she did, his fingers gripping her chin to turn her pallid face towards him for closer, more thorough inspection.

'Let me go, Dante. Please!' Her vividly coloured gaze regarded him with what Dante could only describe as stark, cold terror and it so took him aback that he immediately released her, only to have the door slam soundly shut in his face.

'Bliss! You have to tell me what is going on. Are you keeping something from me? Are you seriously ill? Bliss! I demand to be told the truth this instant!' He heard an unintelligible mumble come from behind the locked door followed very shortly afterwards by the sound of severe retching. His anxiety increasing rapidly, Dante thumped the door with renewed vigour in his furious voice. 'If you do not open the door immediately I will break it down! Do you hear me?'

What he heard was something very like a strained sob, swiftly tamped, then the flushing of the toilet. He cursed very eloquently in fluent Italian, then banged on the door again. 'Bliss! Open this door now! If you don't, I'll—'

But Dante got no further because in the next instant he heard the catch on the other side being released.

Opening the door just a fraction, Bliss gazed back at him, her skin almost ashen, her violet eyes too big for that small heart-shaped face of hers and her lips almost the same colour as her complexion. 'I'm all right,' she told him huskily, her throat clearly strained from her violent retching.

Did she think he was an imbecile? Dante speculated furiously. He hated that she was hiding something from him. Remembering his father telling him how his own mother had hidden her cancer from him until she had barely had a few weeks left to live, Dante felt his stomach recoil with icy dread.

'You must take me for a fool,' he replied coldly, his concern compounded by a terror so great that there was no other inclination than to find out the truth and find it out *now*.

Bliss tried to swallow across the severe pain in her throat and just barely managed it. 'Let me wash my face, then I'll come and join you in the kitchen,' she suggested, her heart squeezing at the evidence of fear in his amazing green eyes. He clearly thought she was suffering from something dire, she realised with a wave of sympathy. The sooner she put him out of his misery, the better. Then he could leave her with equanimity and go back to Italy without ever having to cast another thought in her direction again.

The sudden desire to bawl her eyes out was so strong it was like being knocked off her feet by a tsunami, and Bliss strove with all her might to stave off her tears until she was once again safely ensconced behind a locked bathroom door. But just as she attempted to do exactly that Dante placed his big bronzed hand on her shoulder, turned her gently but firmly around and urged her back into the bathroom. Wordlessly he filled up the enamel basin with warm water, then, wringing out the washcloth at the side of the pink soap dish, he sat Bliss down on the closed toilet seat and proceeded to very gently and carefully wipe her face clean. Twisting her hands together in her lap, Bliss wished she didn't suddenly feel like a small child again because the memory of needing her mother's touch was so raw right then that if she allowed herself to cry just one tear it would be quickly followed by a torrent.

'Thank you.'

'Do you want to brush your teeth?'

At her slight nod, he emptied the water in the basin, lifted a toothbrush out of the enamel holder, squeezed on some toothpaste, then placed it very carefully into her hand. It wasn't the most glamorous thing, Bliss decided—to have the man of your dreams standing in your bathroom watching you brush your teeth after you'd just been at your most vulnerable. She must look like the Angel of Death, she thought suddenly, and her first glance in the mirror above the basin as she brushed confirmed it.

'Better now?'

His expression revealed very little, Bliss reflected nervously as he stood by the door watching her put her toothbrush back in its holder. She hoped he would be leaving soon so that she wouldn't humiliate herself any further in front of him. She'd have to make the story she'd decided upon about a tummy bug sound pretty good if she was going to convince him she wasn't about to die of something horrible. Already he was looking far too suspicious for her peace of mind.

'Much better, thanks. I think I'll go and get dressed now.'

'*Giusto un momento.*'

'Pardon?'

Dante was staring in the direction of the little sea-grass waste-basket at the other side of the basin. When Bliss narrowed her gaze to squint at what had caught his attention, her stomach did a three hundred and sixty-degree roll inside her. Poking out of the top of the basket perched atop some discarded tissue paper was the pregnancy-test stick with its damning evidence clearly visible. Bliss had brought it home with her from Trudy's to take a second and third look at it so that the evidence in front of her could properly sink in. Last night when she'd last used the bathroom she'd finally disposed of it...or thought she had. How could she have known that Dante really meant to stay the night as he had proposed? She had truly believed he would tire of sleeping on her uncomfortable couch and go back to his luxurious hotel suite in Belgravia. How wrong and how stupid could she be?

She clearly *did* take him for a fool! Dante thought furiously as the offending item poking out of the bin continued to fascinate him. He was a thirty-three-year-old, well-travelled, experienced man of the world. Did she not think that he would know what a pregnancy test looked like when he saw one? Now the white face and colourless lips, not to mention the retching, finally started to make sense. Bliss wasn't ill; she was *pregnant!* And if he calculated the timing back to six weeks ago when he was last here—when he had failed to protect her—he did not have a single doubt that the baby was his.

'You are pregnant...*si*?' He pronounced the question in a stunned monotone and Bliss's heart started to race so fast that she had to sit down again on the loo seat.

'I... I was going to tell you.'

'I don't believe you.' Gone was the concern and tenderness that she'd witnessed when he'd washed her face. In its place was a coldness so icy that Bliss decided an arctic wind couldn't be more blisteringly raw.

'Why did you not tell me this yesterday when I arrived? The fact that you did not makes me assume you were going to keep this news from me. Why, Bliss? Were you planning on getting rid of the baby?' Trembling with fury at the very thought, Dante felt a strongly male urge to haul her to her feet and shake the truth out of her right then. He didn't question why he felt so angry and possessive of this unborn child. He only knew that when the realisation had dawned that Bliss was carrying his baby, the joy in his heart had sprung from here to heaven. This child was *his* and he was going to make sure he or she lacked nothing. There would never be issues about not belonging or feeling second best, as Dante had often suffered throughout his own childhood and adolescence.

As his words sank in Bliss's expression turned to anger. 'Of course I wasn't planning on doing such a thing! How can you even *think* that when you don't know the first thing about me?'

Dante's lips looked cold and tight. 'But you *were* going to keep this news from me? You would have let me walk out the door without telling me you were carrying my child. It *is* my child, isn't it, Bliss? I do not believe you could have turned to another man so soon after we made love.'

He'd got that right. Bliss sighed inwardly. At least he wasn't accusing her of sleeping with anyone else. Still, his obvious Italian male pride had kicked in, and he clearly knew his passionate attentions would put any other man who attempted the same firmly in the shade. It made Bliss grow hot even now to remember them.

'I only found out yesterday. I just thought I had a cold

and a tummy upset. I never imagined I might be—be pregnant.' She knew the hectic colour that rose in her cheeks belied her words. Now she was consumed with embarrassment and guilt at thinking she could fool herself into denying the true fact of the matter, as well as feeling bad that she had obviously lied to Dante. But everything had happened so quickly…so unexpectedly. Neither of them had taken time to think about the consequences of what they'd done.

Because she had grown up with chaos, Bliss had consciously striven to try and counteract that effect in her adult life by trying to instil some order; some *control*. But she hadn't been thinking about control or self-restraint when she'd given herself to Dante in such an abandoned way that morning, she was ashamed to realise. Instead she had allowed herself to get carried away in the thrill of a moment that she'd convinced herself only happened once in a lifetime, and now she was facing the dire consequences of her actions.

'And now we have to talk about what we are going to do, no?'

He said this in such a way that Bliss instinctively knew he had already made his mind up about what action to take. Her spine started to tingle with indignation before she even replied.

'I'm keeping the child,' she said firmly, lifting her chin to emphasise the point. 'You can, of course, have visitation rights. As long as you let me know when you're coming I won't make things difficult.'

'No!'

Dante's head had started to spin at the idea that Bliss would keep the child and shut him out. Just as he had been shut out as a small boy, made to feel different, as if he weren't worthy of the love others received. And how would Bliss fare on her own as a single parent? His gaze swept the clean but tired-looking bathroom, seeing all the things that made it clear to him that her lifestyle was nowhere near as comfortable or as affluent as his own, and Dante knew he didn't want her to endure such a struggle. A little muscle throbbed at the side of his temple as he tried to establish some command over his feelings, but his efforts were demolished in an instant when he suddenly thought about the very real possibility of Bliss meeting someone else who would help raise his child. What if they did not treat the baby right? Or, God help them—if they were *cruel* in any way? Dante couldn't bear the terrifying thought of history repeating itself.

'No?' Feeling her body start to tremble at the rage in his eyes, Bliss smoothed the flimsy material of her wrap down over her knees and linked her hands nervously together in her lap. Squaring those magnificently broad shoulders of his as if he was preparing himself for a verbal war, Dante sliced his hand through the air to reiterate his objection more passionately.

'Do not talk to me about visitation rights, Bliss, or you will find yourself in court up against the best lawyers money can buy! I will not be told I need to have *permission* to visit my own flesh and blood! I intend to be a proper father to this child we have made together and I also intend for you to be a proper mother. To achieve this end you will marry me and come to live with me in Italy. There is no other option to which I am open, *comprende*?'

Bliss's mouth dropped open. She could hardly believe what he was saying. When they'd parted last, he'd indicated that they might see each other from time to time, but, although she'd allowed herself to hope that he meant it, she hadn't honestly really believed she would ever see him again. Now she had and he was proposing to marry her because he'd found out she was pregnant!

She leapt to her feet, her expression agitated. He couldn't *really* want to marry her, could he? Wasn't he acting purely out of a sense of obligation or, even worse, guilt? Marriage on such terms could be nothing but disastrous in Bliss's book.

'Now, wait just a minute here. I don't want to get married! I told you about my feelings on marriage when we first met. You can't force me, Dante. I am a free woman and I can make my own decisions about what I will or will not do in my life!'

'Think about what you are so eager to refuse, Bliss.' Meeting her defiant, disturbed gaze, Dante only knew that he had to drive home the fact that he was deadly serious about marrying her. He would not give up the idea of being a proper father to his child without a fight. He would not be shut out again. 'How hard will it be for you to raise a child on your own? I am a very wealthy man and I am willing to assume my proper responsibility regarding this situation. In my opinion it would be extremely foolish for you to turn your back on the chance for our child to have a proper upbringing with two parents fully committed to his welfare. I am right, no?'

As she wrapped her arms around her chest and stared at him mutely as if the answer to his question had completely deserted her Dante pushed home his advantage with his heart throbbing heavily inside his chest.

'You must put aside your reluctance to marry in favour of doing what is best for the child. Do not worry, you will be more than amply provided for and taken care of. I have a luxurious house in Rome and an equally magnificent apartment in Milan. You will never again have to do work that you despise. Is that not worth the *sacrifice* of marrying me?'

God help her, where was this leading? Now it seemed that she had goaded him too far, because he was clearly taking umbrage at the fact that she thought marriage to him could only be a sacrifice. He had no idea of the intensity of her feelings for him at all. No idea that if she hadn't fallen pregnant, she would have secretly loved to have been courted by him. Her heart would have jumped for joy at the mere idea that he might consider choosing her as his girlfriend—but now all chances of some kind of romantic courtship were dashed for good. Now Dante only wanted to marry Bliss to do the right thing for his child. He hadn't even mentioned having any kind of feelings for her at all. Disaster beckoned with a capital 'D'.

'Why did you come back, Dante?' Her emotions raw, Bliss bit down heavily on her tender lower lip, feeling far too vulnerable and exposed in her flimsy wrap to have any kind of advantage at all. Now wasn't the time for vulnerability. Now was the time to act with some strength. But with Dante's coolly emerald eyes pinning her to the floor, and he in contrast looking so clearly in charge and self-possessed, all Bliss wanted to do right now was to escape his gaze as quickly as she could. She needed time on her own to calm herself and think through the situation more rationally, because it was almost impossible to think straight with Dante in the same room as her.

To her intense surprise he grinned sexily in answer to the question she'd asked, further scattering all possibility of calmness to the four winds.

'I very much liked making love to you, Bliss. When a man makes such a deep connection to a woman…of course he wants to come back.'

'So you came back because you liked the sex?' Biting down on her lip even harder, Bliss couldn't prevent the hotly sensuous ache that suddenly made her limbs feel treacherously weak. His heated, piercing gaze deliberately lingering on her body as if he was mentally peeling back her clothing to reveal her naked skin underneath, Dante shrugged as if the answer to that was obvious.

'Do not pretend you are offended, *innamorata*. You are a beautiful, sensuous woman with hot, passionate blood in her veins. At least that will be one part of our marriage that should work beautifully...*sì*?'

Her embarrassed gaze sliding quickly away from his, Bliss was consumed with both doubt and anticipation at the idea of being married to a man like Dante di Andrea and sharing his bed. Then, almost as soon as she'd let the idea play out in her mind, she realised with a shock what she was contemplating. She didn't want to get married at all! She knew that, had always known it. None of the examples of the married state she'd known had lent themselves to persuading Bliss to do the same. She had to look no further than her parents' ultimately disastrous union. Dante meant well, Bliss was certain, but this was no proposal born out of love—he had only proposed marriage because he felt duty-bound, because of the child she was expecting. How many marriages had started off in the same way and fallen at the first hurdle?

'I told you, Dante, I don't want to get married...not now, not *ever*. We can both still be responsible parents without being married. Lots of people—'

Exasperated and angry that she would not easily come round to his point of view, Dante finally lost his temper.

'I do not care what other people do or not do! I only care what I, Dante di Andrea, must do! I have fathered a child with you and I take full and complete responsibility for that. Do you think I would go home to Italy to my family and tell them I have abandoned the mother of my expected child in England? I have a good reputation amongst my peers and my family. Do you imagine I would willingly jeopardise that because you are acting so irresponsibly?'

'I'm not acting irresponsibly! For goodness' sake, Dante, think about what you're suggesting! We hardly know each other, yet you're expecting me to marry you and go to Italy with you just like that!'

'We will remedy the fact we do not yet know each other well by living together. I will take some time off from my work and spend it with you. You will not want for anything, I promise you.'

'I—I have a life here, Dante. I'm starting a new job on Monday.'

He honed in on her statement with ruthless intensity, like an eagle swooping down on his terrified prey. 'What kind of life do you have here, Bliss? You have no family to support you. Tragic as that is, I am only too willing to make up for the deficit. I am offering to marry you and give you a much better, higher standard of living in Italy than you have here. If your mother was alive and you knew where to contact your father, do you think they would be happy that their daughter gave birth to an illegitimate child and struggled on welfare to keep a roof over their heads?'

That telling little muscle at the side of his temple throbbed furiously, illustrating to Bliss that his anger was white hot. But she wouldn't let his superior attitude railroad her into a decision she was unhappy with—no matter how much she might secretly fantasise it could all work out for the best.

'My parents were far too wrapped up in their own

problems to worry about me, so I don't suppose it would have made much difference to them whether I stayed here or moved to Timbucktu!' Her distress multiplied with every word she uttered. Brushing back her hair with trembling fingers, she exhaled a long, slow breath to try and hold back feelings that were akin to an open wound being mercilessly rubbed with salt.

Recognising the relentlessly bleak expression in her eyes as the kind of pain that came from enduring a hurt that ran fathoms deep, Dante sighed and shook his head, reining in his temper. He didn't mean to add to her mental suffering. All he wanted to do was make her see that he was genuinely promising to be the best husband and father he could be. Surely she couldn't prefer to live here in almost poverty than come to Italy with him and live a life of luxury and ease? Already they had a powerful physical attraction for one another. Dante might not be able to fully commit his heart to this woman, but in every other way she would not have reason to find him lacking.

'I am sorry.'

'Don't be.' Shrugging carelessly, Bliss tried not to flinch from the compassion she saw in his eyes. She didn't want his pity. Neither did she want his help—not if it came at the price of her independence. 'Stuff like that happens to people all of the time. I'm not the only one who didn't have the perfect textbook childhood.'

'That may be so...' Dante held her gaze, almost imprisoning it by force of will... 'But *our bambino* will not suffer in the same way. He or she will have two parents that will put the child first...*always.*'

'I don't doubt your sincerity, Dante, but—'

'No buts.' He looked fierce. A warrior in full charge on the battlefield could not have looked fiercer. 'I will take care of things from now on. You no longer have to do everything on your own. And neither do you need a job to go to on Monday. Ring them up and tell them you have changed your mind.'

As Bliss stared at him in disbelief he threw her another highly charged glance that said clearly, *And if you don't, I will do it for you.*

CHAPTER EIGHT

His telephone call at an end, Dante found Bliss in her bedroom folding up some clothing on the bed, her slender shoulders hunched and her back to him as he entered. His instinctive reaction was to offer her comfort, but he thought that she probably wouldn't welcome such a commodity from him right now, and repressed the urge. Her feelings had no doubt been in turmoil since discovering she was pregnant, and now he had swept back into her life again, proposing to be her husband, and all her plans for a single, independent life had been turned on their head.

Dante surprised himself at how passionate he was about the idea of marrying her. Especially when for so long he had almost despaired of finding the right woman. There had been a lot of women in his life and he would be the first to admit that sometimes he took their often overbearing attention for granted. But there had never been another woman who had made him feel as if he wanted to stake some kind of claim on her exclusively, or whom he could imagine spending the rest of his life with. But then, his need to safeguard Bliss Maguire from harm or distress had been growing stronger in him moment by moment since he had learned she was pregnant with his baby. Doubly so since she had reluctantly revealed more of the circumstances of her family life.

'That is settled, then. You are moving in with me to my family's hotel in Belgravia this afternoon. Just pack a few clothes; anything else you need, the hotel can provide for you.'

'Excuse me?'

As she turned to face him Bliss's expression was one of disbelief and protest. 'Forgive me if I've been mistakenly labouring under the impression that I have free will. Let me remind you, Dante, that I don't have to answer to you and neither are you in charge of my life! I am not coming with you to Belgravia or Italy or anywhere else you so high-handedly dictate to me! I am an independent woman and I want to stay in my own home—however abhorrent it may seem to you.' Tension snaked across her slender back like an iron rod, almost making it hard to breathe. 'It may not be anywhere near as luxurious or desirable as Tatiana's apartment in Chelsea, but it's my home nonetheless, and I love it! Nothing has been agreed between us yet and nothing will be if you continue to take that dictatorial tone with me!'

Letting her furious words bounce off him like so many cotton-wool balls aimed from a distance, Dante shrugged in a manner that was undoubtedly arrogant but made no apology for it, not when he knew for certain that his actions were unquestionably right.

'I do not understand why you should be so offended. I am merely acting out of concern for you and our unborn child. You will be far more comfortable in our hotel than you could possibly be here. I am not trying to denigrate your home in any way when I say this, but be honest with yourself, Bliss—this is not a suitable area for a young woman who is pregnant to live in. I would be failing in my duty as your husband-to-be and father of your child if I did not do something to rectify that.'

'Lots of young single pregnant woman live in this area, for your information!'

'Perhaps.' His gaze narrowing meaningfully, Dante paused as if to add weight to his words. 'But you will not be single for long, Bliss. I intend our marriage to take place as quickly as it can possibly be arranged. That is what my mother and father would naturally want, and that is what *I* want too.'

'Really.' Her smooth brow furrowing in resentment, Bliss folded her arms furiously across her chest, staring down the handsome black-haired male with the devastating green eyes as if the sheer force of her anger alone could render him temporarily speechless. 'Do you know how bloody arrogant that sounds? What about what *I* want, Dante? I'm the one who's carrying this baby. It's *my* body that it's growing inside, not yours, your father's or your mother's!'

'Enough!' His glance sharp as a blade buried in ice, Dante held up his hand as if to slice off the end of her angry tirade. 'You are letting your emotions override your ability to see what is good for you. This insistence on independence is ridiculous under the circumstances! You have no family to offer you support, so from now on *I* will take full responsibility for your well-being. I suggest you take some time out to think things over more rationally and also to get some rest. I have some business to attend to back at the hotel, after which I will come back and collect you.'

Biting back a further retort, Bliss wondered if it had ever occurred to this man that not everyone in the world believed his word was law. Her strong need to be in control of her own destiny was silently kicking and screaming at his clear intention to take over her life and tell her what was best for her. Yet at the same time how could her secret heart deny that the prospect of being

married to this handsome, sexy, highly honourable man
held some appeal?

Right now she was mentally and physically so fatigued
that she hardly trusted herself to make the right decision
about her own and her baby's future anyway. Some time
on her own to think things through 'rationally'—Bliss
almost choked on the word—wouldn't be a bad thing,
she had to agree.

'Okay. I'll do as you suggest, for now.' She dropped
down onto the edge of her bed, not caring that she'd sat
on the newly laundered clothes she'd just folded, feeling
as if she could fall asleep right where she sat. 'But don't
count on me coming back with you, Dante. You might
think I should jump at the chance but there's a lot at
stake here for me. My independence, for one thing.'

To her surprise, his compelling mouth curved into a
smile that was akin to the most lustfully tempting dessert
on an à la carte menu, and suddenly Bliss didn't feel so
tired any more. She felt as if she'd just been given a shot
of adrenaline straight into her heart.

'I have no doubt you will make the right decision. You
will not wish to deny our baby the right to a father and
a start in life that isn't one of struggle and hardship,
surely?'

Of course she wouldn't! But Bliss was scared—no,
correct that, *terrified*—at what marriage to Dante di
Andrea might mean. It wasn't just about her imagined
loss of independence or her cynical belief that marriages
never worked out—it was also about the possible lack of
control over her own life. She'd already gleaned that
Dante was more than a little old-fashioned in his attitude
to women. In his hallowed sphere, where wealth
abounded, men were very definitely the ones in charge.
Would she be expected to be some kind of appendage to

his more important, busy life, or would he take her needs and wants into consideration too? Bliss couldn't know for sure, so she was naturally wary. But, even with all her doubts, right now his invitation to move in with him to his family's hotel with a view to eventually moving to Italy sounded almost more seductive than she could bear.

It was incontrovertible fact that she was going to have a baby and she had to consider the child's future as well as her own. Did she *really* want her child to have a poor beginning with a mother who didn't even have a proper career to support them both, let alone a job that would provide enough money for her to pay for a child-minder when she had to go back to it? Bliss's heart gave a little skip of fear. She'd seen the young single mums who lived in the same block of flats as she did, their faces lined with care and worry and old before their time. Was that what she wanted for herself? Dante's proposal deserved proper consideration before she dismissed it so easily— just because she'd sworn she'd never get married. She also hadn't planned on having children, but fate obviously had other ideas in store for her.

Her tongue gliding across her upper lip to moisten it, Bliss couldn't help shivering as she regarded Dante across the room.

'I'll let you have my decision when you return. I promise I'll think carefully about it. In the meantime, I really need to put my head down.' Too slow to smother a yawn, she waited expectantly for him to go. But Dante didn't move from the spot where he stood. His libido had just been sensually tormented to an agonising degree by the sight of that little gesture Bliss had so casually made with her tongue. Now he honestly didn't feel like doing anything else except maybe suggesting that he join her in bed.

'Okay. I will be back soon.' He made himself turn around and head for the front door before he simply lost the will to even think of leaving.

He ordered flowers to be placed in every room. Huge bunches of scented blooms perfumed the air as Dante restlessly walked across wide expanses of deeply luxurious carpet, his hawk-eyed glance sifting out any imperfections immediately and giving clear, precise instructions to the man at his side for whatever had offended his eye to be instantly remedied. The hotel manager Guido Vaccaro, a young, impeccably turned out graduate from Milan who had worked for the di Andrea hotel in Sardinia, made hurried notes on a little pad he carried with him, speaking with Dante in gesticulating Italian as if the two of them were of one mind together. When it came to style and, surprisingly, even old-fashioned grandeur, Guido's taste was faultless, and Dante wanted both the hotel and the sumptuous family suite to impress Bliss so much that she would not hesitate to stay. Suddenly the fact that he was going to become a father had become the most important thing in the world to Dante and he wanted the mother of his child to be totally confident of his desire to be a proper parent.

He also wanted to place the beautiful and sensitive Bliss Maguire amidst the loveliness she deserved—somewhere that would do justice to her beauty and sensitivity. When he thought of her carrying his child, alone and struggling to make ends meet living in that grey, depressing block of flats…the idea was anathema to him, an abomination not to be endured.

Recalling Bliss's comment about rich, pampered women with bathrooms full of perfume, he told Guido to ask his assistant Nathalie to get a cab to Selfridges in

Oxford Street and purchase at least half a dozen fragrances to put in what would be Dante and Bliss's shared marble bathroom. He mentioned a couple of classic fragrances he enjoyed women wearing and also instructed Nathalie to buy some newer, more modern ones as well so that Bliss would be spoiled for choice.

Once the suite had been brought up to the matchless standard that Dante expected, with not a cushion or a flower petal or a piece of furniture remotely out of place, he went into his private office to telephone his parents. The call he made would be quickly followed by another to Tatiana, his sister—after which, Dante would order a special dinner for himself and Bliss; a dinner that they would enjoy in the privacy of their exquisite suite of rooms, alone.

Tatiana's shriek at the other end of the line almost pierced Dante's eardrum. 'You are going to marry Bliss Maguire? The girl who came here to look after Renata? Oh Dante, she is wonderful! At last you have found someone you can love with all your heart. I am so happy for you!'

His sister's comment almost winded him, so as well as a perforated eardrum his ability to breathe was nearly compromised as well. He did not love Bliss with all his heart. He didn't know if he was capable of loving anyone with all his heart—except maybe members of his immediate family, and even then he suspected he didn't give any of them his whole heart. The prospect seemed far too dangerous. But Dante knew he cared for Bliss. In fact it quite took him aback to realise just how much he had come to care for her in such a short space of time. And now that she was going to have his baby... Dante let the thought seep through to his very bones, feeling warmth touch all the cold places in his body that were often deprived of inner sunshine…in time he would come to care for her even more.

'I had a similar reception from *Mamma* and *Papà*.'

Allowing himself a brief, satisfied smile, Dante glanced at the little vase of freesias Nathalie had placed on his desk, his senses captivated for a moment by their simple loveliness and heady scent. He'd chosen all the flowers that decorated the suite himself, and it was his cherished hope that Bliss would be just as enraptured by their beauty as he was. 'I did not realise that my getting married would engender such enthusiasm from you all.'

There was a distinct pause at the other end of the line and Dante heard the delicate rush of breath that came from a clearly thoughtful Tatiana. 'I cannot believe you do not know how much your happiness means to all of us, my brother. It makes me very sad to think that you do not value yourself as much as we do.'

His sister's astute comment caught Dante on the raw. His hard jaw tightening, he fielded the wave of melancholy that suddenly welled up inside him with almost angry determination. He would not expose his secret weakness to anyone—not even his baby sister. After his father, Dante was the head of the family. No one should know that he hardly felt deserving of such a serious responsibility. His mixed blood, as well as his grandparents' rejection of his father, had seared him to the core all his life. Even Antonio did not know how much these facts burdened his eldest son. Nor would he know, if Dante had any say in the matter.

'There is something else you should know, *sorella piccola*. I am also to be a father.'

'Bliss is expecting a *bambino*? When? How? But that means you must have got together about the time she came to help with little Renny? Oh, Dante…is this a mistake? Do you really want to marry this girl after all?'

Alarmed at the distress in his sister's voice, Dante did not waste a second in alleviating her worst fears for him. '*Sì*, Tatiana. I really do want to marry Bliss. This is no mistake, I promise you.'

'I am relieved…and excited! So much sadness and now this amazing thing has happened. *Mamma* and I will get together and make sure she looks absolutely beautiful on her wedding day. When is it to be?'

He had already enquired about a civil marriage in the UK and the soonest it could be done was in fifteen days' time. All Dante had to do now was convince Bliss to produce the necessary documents so that he could arrange things. He prayed she would not be difficult about this. All he wanted was a chance to be a family and assume his proper responsibility to his child. Surely she would want that too?

'As soon as all the details have been arranged I will come and talk to you. There are other things I also need to discuss…your future being one of them, Tatiana.'

'*Mamma* has indicated that you and *Papà* have been talking. I know it has something to do with me and Renata coming back to Italy to live, *sì*?'

'You are not against the idea?'

'No.' Her voice growing soft, Tatiana sighed. 'Since losing Matt I know that I want to have my family around me more than anything. So after you tell me all the news about you and Bliss, we will discuss my coming back home.'

Dante couldn't help but feel relieved that at least one of his difficult tasks had apparently been accomplished with more ease than he had expected. Now all he had to do was convince Bliss that *her* best option was to become his wife.

Staring at her opened suitcase on the opulent sleigh-style bed with its plush burgundy counterpane in the centre of the luxurious bedroom, Bliss took several moments to get her bearings. Was this really happening to her? Until yesterday she had been working as an ordinary assistant behind a beauty counter in a large department store, living in a small rented flat on a dingy ex-council estate. And now…now she had moved into this unbelievably gracious and beautiful hotel in Belgravia, and was going to become the wife of a wealthy Italian hotelier. Not only his wife, but the mother of his child too. Such a dramatic change in circumstances would surely make the most level-headed person think that they'd woken up in Wonderland?

Her tongue clicking against her teeth, Bliss shook off her reverie and found her gaze inadvertently colliding with the dressing-table mirror opposite the bed. A jab of dismay jolted through her. The shadows beneath her eyes were so dark that she looked as if she'd just seen the light of day after being locked up in a windowless prison for forty years! As she critically examined the rest of her features, she also concluded that her rich dark hair had definitely lost its lustre since she'd realised she was pregnant. Whether it was hormones or just general anxiety to blame, she couldn't tell. All she knew was that she very definitely didn't feel at her best right now, and that was partly why she had caved in so easily to Dante's forthright demand that she take up residence with him at his family's hotel.

When he'd come back for her and again persuasively listed all the reasons for her becoming his wife—first and foremost to give the baby the best future possible—Bliss had finally concluded that it was pointless to fight something so impossibly hard to resist. She wanted the best possible future for her baby too and, to tell the truth, how could she also resist a taste of luxury and a chance to let go of responsibility when all her life she had been longing for just that? Her whole life had been too overshadowed by the weight of adult responsibilities from far too young an age, and sometimes, Bliss mused, that was surely the reason she felt so mentally fatigued most of the time. Too fatigued to really make the effort required in pursuing a career that would generate some better prospects.

And besides, it appeared that Dante really wanted to do this. He *wanted* to take responsibility for the coming child, and he *wanted* Bliss to be his wife. Okay, so they weren't in love…but they didn't exactly hate each other either, did they? Even in her newly pregnant condition Bliss only had to glance his way just briefly to feel lightheaded and feverish. She was so acutely sensitive to his presence that her limbs were immediately deluged by a deliciously silky weakness whenever he appeared, which destroyed her ability to think about anything but desiring him in the most carnal way…

She registered the sound of the door opening behind her with a guilty jolt, silently marvelling that even the soft snick of the catch sounded luxurious and expensive to her hypersensitive hearing.

'You do not have to unpack now if you are feeling tired. Leave it and I will get a chambermaid to come up and do it for you.'

He had taken off his suit jacket at last and partially rolled up the sleeves on his crisp white shirt to expose his bronzed forearms. His more casual appearance did no more to help Bliss relax than when he was dressed formally. Every molecule in the air seemed to react as if it had received an immense electrical charge when Dante walked into the room and the portion that she sucked into her lungs, doubly so. But although his angular handsome face gave very little away and his riveting green eyes were just as intensely attractive as ever, Bliss couldn't help noticing that his compelling mouth was showing definite signs of strain. As if he wasn't as sure of himself as he liked to project.

'It's okay. I'm happy to do it. I was just—just getting my bearings.' Smiling tentatively, Bliss smoothed down her hair, feeling about as confident as a five-year-old sneaking into her mother's wardrobe to play 'dress up'. It would definitely not work in her favour to let Dante see her own signs of strain, she decided. At no point did she want to give him an advantage and prove that she couldn't take care of herself. She also couldn't help wondering under the circumstances if he expected her to share this wonderful, opulent bed with him tonight. Her heart skittered alarmingly at the thought.

'You have everything you need?' His sharp glance around the room told her this was for some reason important to him and, finding her head alarmingly bereft of a clear thought, all Bliss could manage was a faint nod. Besides, she wasn't used to anyone asking her if she had everything she needed. That was usually *her* job.

'Perhaps you should lie down for a little while before dinner? I have arranged for us to eat in the sitting room this evening. We can talk undisturbed and you do not have to worry about looking your best in the dining room. You can relax.'

Knowing that Dante probably thought she looked like something the cat had dragged in and that even a full service by a top make-up artist couldn't effect a miracle, Bliss felt her spirits plummet sharply. Was that why he had filled the bathroom with all manner of exotic and expensive perfumes? Was it a not-so-subtle reminder that, now she was with him, she had to assume the guise of one of those rich, pampered women she'd so despised, with nothing better to do all day long but spend endless hours titivating their appearance for some man? The thought made her suddenly furious.

'You mean you don't want me embarrassing you looking like this—that's what you mean, isn't it? And by the way, I noticed your little hint with all the perfume. For your information, it makes me heave. It's bad enough that I'm surrounded by it all day at work without being expected to practically bathe in it to make myself more attractive! And while we're on the subject, I don't need incentives to reach any kind of decision about the future. Your wealth and your ability to buy me things don't impress me.'

Feeling wounded and uncomfortably emotional, she cursed her wayward pregnancy hormones, then lifted a sweater from her suitcase and held it to her chest. She should have made more of an effort with her appearance, she scolded herself. God knew, it wasn't a lot to ask, was it? Jeans and a pink tee shirt with 'Love' written on the front in bold white lettering were fine for relaxing at home in, but this was Dante's family hotel and, if the sumptuous Italianate décor was anything to go by, it had an equally imposing dress code. Bliss knew she hadn't imagined the snooty glance from the exquisitely attired receptionist on the front desk when she had walked through the doors with Dante by her side earlier.

'You think I am embarrassed by you and at the same time trying to buy you with my gifts?' Scowling, Dante walked over to her side. He took the sweater out of her agitated hands and threw it unceremoniously back down on top of her other clothes, then slid warm but hard, commanding fingers beneath her chin, raising it a little so that her startled gaze had no choice but to meet with his. 'Why would you say such an outrageous thing? Why would you even think it? You are the mother-to-be of my child. The perfume was evidently a mistake under the circumstances, but I did not mean to offend you and neither am I trying to impress you with my wealth or coerce you into anything. The idea did not even cross my mind, and it is insulting to me! It is fortunate that you are carrying my child, Bliss, because if you were not, I would not find it so easy to hold back my temper!'

Seeing the sudden alarm in her eyes, Dante released her with a frustrated sigh. He didn't want to scare her. All he wanted to do was get her to see that he had her and the baby's welfare at heart. That was his prime motivation for bringing her here to his family's hotel. Any other woman of his acquaintance would have basked in all the attention. The fact that Bliss remained unimpressed by Dante's wealth and position reminded him that she was worlds apart from the clinging gold-diggers that it was often his misfortune to attract, and his anger suddenly drained away. More softly, he continued, 'You are also young and very beautiful...*molto bella*, as we say in Italy. Of this I should be embarrassed?'

Bliss moved her gaze and stared at the cleft in his chin, trying desperately to convince herself that it was only a common or garden dimple—not a teasing thumbprint left by an admiring angel when he was born, as her wild imagination insisted it was. The trouble was, Dante couldn't help being so effortlessly gorgeous and Bliss knew, no matter how many times he paid her lavish compliments and called her *'molto bella'*, she was never going to be in the same league. But now he was regarding her with a sexy, knowing glance, and as her violet eyes shaded to dark, any thoughts of feeling less than good were totally banished beneath the hotly smouldering gaze that Dante was currently subjecting her to.

'I should have given more thought to my appearance, perhaps, but I am not used to moving in the kind of social circles you do, Dante,' she conceded softly, her anger dissipating.

Instead of answering her directly, Dante let loose a smile that turned Bliss's insides to melting wax. Dropping his gaze to the front of her pink tee shirt, he traced the 'L' of the word 'Love' with his finger, deliberately lingering over the part of the letter that was nearest to the peak of her breast with idle enjoyment. 'I like the way you dress, *innamorata*. It is young and sexy, just like you. And isn't love what we all need more of? Besides…' The cadence of his voice lowering to almost gravel, Dante fixed her with such an openly devouring glance that for a moment Bliss felt as if she were standing on the deck of a ship in a storm because her emotions were lurching so violently '…I am more interested in what you look like undressed than clothed, if you want to know the truth.'

'But, Dante, I—'

'Shh.' Silencing her with a finger across her lips, Dante cupped the weight of her breast fully in his palm and sensuously coaxed Bliss's already tightening nipple to pucker even more tightly. The violent connection to her womb was like a small incendiary exploding inside her and her teeth came down on her lip and almost drew blood.

'Please don't do that!'

Seeing her lips tremble and her beautiful eyes darken to the most seductive, deepest violet Dante had ever seen, he knew it was an impossible request. He was so hot for her, so turned on by her innocent, unaffected beauty, that it physically hurt to try and switch off his growing desire for her. But then he remembered the growing baby in her womb and realised that she probably needed a rest more than sexual attention from her amorous husband-to-be. Just for tonight, Dante vowed, he would not make demands on her body; he would let her rest as much as possible.

But *tomorrow* night…from tomorrow he would persuade her that making love would be very good for them both. Not just good, but necessary. Knowing he hadn't imagined the hot flare of excitement in her gaze when he had touched her just now, Dante didn't doubt for one moment that he could persuade her.

CHAPTER NINE

DANTE waited for Bliss to appear from the bathroom before he presented her with his plans for the day. He'd heard her about an hour ago succumbing to another bout of sickness and he had paced the short corridor outside the bathroom intermittently since then, his stomach muscles so cramped that the tension in them hurt. He was more on edge than he would be in any business negotiation he entered into, because at least in that situation he could determine the outcome. Failure was anathema to him and he *always* came out on top. But Bliss being pregnant, and Dante not being able to influence the toll it took on her body, were another matter altogether.

Not for the first time that morning, he wished that his mother Isabella were close by because Dante was certain she would be a ministering angel to Bliss in her distress. It grieved him sorely that Bliss did not have her own mother to call upon and made him even more determined that the path that lay ahead of her would be as smooth as he could make it. Which was why their first task of the day was to visit Sandrine Lantain in Harley Street and have Bliss get a thorough health check.

'You're all dressed up. Are you going out?'

He was no more dressed up than usual in another gorgeous suit that couldn't help but enhance the already spectacular physique of the man who wore it. But it seemed to Bliss that every time she set eyes on Dante anew, it became increasingly impossible to think straight around him. Could anyone blame her for coming out with inane remarks under the circumstances?

'We are going out together. I am taking you to see a friend of the family's in Harley Street.'

Aware that his gaze was checking every detail of her appearance—no doubt for flaws—Bliss was slightly bolstered by the fact that she'd made a better effort with her outfit today. She'd matched a recently purchased light green cardigan with fitted boot-cut denims and a brown woven belt. Keeping her make-up to a 'barely there' application of eyeliner, blush and some raspberry-coloured lip gloss, she'd taken more time than usual fixing her hair and was at least feeling reasonably satisfied with her efforts. But alarm bells started ringing when Dante mentioned Harley Street. Her soft brows drew quizzically together. 'And who might this friend be? He wouldn't be a doctor, by any chance, would he?'

'You need to have a proper physical now that you are pregnant.'

'I'll go and see my own doctor, thank you.'

Ducking her glance away from his, Bliss realised she was still self-conscious about discussing the intimate details of her pregnancy with Dante, even though he was the baby's father. By nature she had always been a very private person and now, finding herself in a situation where her fiercely guarded privacy was being threatened, she couldn't help but feel under attack.

'Sandrine Lantain is an obstetrician, Bliss. She looked after Tatiana when she was pregnant with Renata. I want you to go and see her and have a proper examination. I am concerned that you are so sick every morning and I would like to get her advice.'

'It's normal to suffer with morning sickness when you're pregnant!'

'How many children have you had that you are now such an expert?'

His sarcasm hurt and Bliss turned away. She nearly jumped through the ceiling when he took hold of her arm to irritably compel her full, undivided attention. 'You may have been used to being less than diligent in taking proper care of yourself until now. But now that you are going to be the mother of my child, you will discover that things are going to be very different.'

There was a little tightening around the eyes as he said this and Bliss felt as though she'd just been chastised with the pointed end of a red-hot needle. 'Go to hell!' Wrenching back her arm, her fury at being spoken to as if she were a dense adolescent who needed to have the error of her ways pointed out almost rendering her speechless, Bliss stepped back unthinkingly and cracked her head against the wall. She was doubly annoyed at being so accident-prone, and her expression was petulant as she rubbed at her scalp to ease the pain. 'Now see what you've done! Why can't you just go away and leave me alone? I never asked you to come back. I'm going to bring up this baby on my own without your help and there's not a damn thing you can do about it! *I'm* the one giving him life and *I'm* the one who will be responsible for his welfare!'

'Over my dead body.' The four short words were spoken with a deadly seriousness that made Bliss's blood run cold, dousing her rebellion as swiftly as if a bucket of ice water had been thrown over her. Within just a few chilling seconds she had quickly learned that Dante di Andrea was not a man who would suffer dismissal or contempt in any shape or form. Especially not when the future of his unborn child was at stake. 'I will grant you lenience in your truculent manner towards me up to a point, Bliss. But once that point is crossed, you will find out that my retaliation will be swift and merciless.'

Now that he most definitely had her full, wide-eyed attention, Dante continued. 'You will think twice about challenging me in such a reckless way. Any more talk of bringing up our child on your own and I will demonstrate that there is *plenty* I can do to stop you. I will have you in court so quickly that it will be you who will be negotiating visitation rights with me! *Comprende?* Make no mistake that I mean every word I say.'

Biting back her fear and resentment, Bliss glared mutely back at him, her defiant lavender eyes speaking volumes. As if to rub salt into her wounds, Dante smiled at her with the complacent, self-satisfied glance of a man who was very much used to getting his own way and, in fact, expected it.

'Now I am going to take you to see Sandrine. I have already made an appointment. Make yourself ready and we will go. I have a driver waiting out front.'

About to open her mouth in protest, Bliss found herself staring at Dante's broad, suited back as he turned and deliberately walked away as if any further discussion on the matter was now obsolete.

'Hey! Don't you dare just walk away from me as if the subject was closed!'

Clearly unimpressed by her futile display of annoyance, he turned and regarded her with a lazy—bordering on arrogant—smile.

'It is, *innamorata*. I am afraid you are just going to have to accept that my word is final.'

Putting her clothes back on behind the screen, Bliss's fingers shook slightly as she did up the intricately woven buttons on her cardigan. Sandrine Lantain had been lovely. Very professional yet warm, and Bliss hadn't failed to notice the way her blue eyes had lit up when Dante had walked into her consulting room. So what was new? What woman wouldn't just love to bask in his exclusive attention for even a moment? Her stomach reiterated the rhetorical question with a very definite jolt. Now he was out there with the lovely Sandrine, no doubt discussing every single detail of his wife-to-be's pregnancy and no doubt—because the obstetrician was a family friend—trying to explain how he had found himself in such an untenable position with a woman he hardly knew.

For a moment Bliss wished there were a back way out so that she could escape before Dante realised she was gone—back to her undesirable flat and the life she had had before she had ever set eyes on him. Then she told herself to calm down and think seriously for a moment about what she was evidently so eager to throw away. She might be in the dark about his true feelings towards her, but one thing was clear—Dante was apparently determined to fulfil his role as a husband and father to the letter. She sighed softly. Marriage to him could not possibly be worse than facing the prospect of single parenthood, struggling to make ends meet for herself and her child. If Dante was prepared to try and make a go of things, then the least Bliss could do was to be equally committed. Maybe in time, when he got to know her better, he might find out that he hadn't made such a bad choice after all?

Feeling the weight of what felt like a bowling ball in the pit of her stomach, Bliss returned to the consulting room, a deliberately fixed smile on her face as she approached the obstetrician and Dante either side of the big oak desk.

'Are you okay?' The expression on his handsome face revealing concern, Dante stood up as Bliss entered the room and drew back a second chair next to his own for her to sit down.

'Yes, I'm fine.' She deliberately kept her voice terse to show him she hadn't forgiven him for the dictatorial way he'd spoken to her earlier, but, feeling the touch of his hand warm her through the soft wool of her cardigan, Bliss realised that she had no defences where this man was concerned. Even her resentment did not prevent the torrid rush of need that pulsed through her body every time they made contact, however slight. Knowing that, she felt her already undeniable sense of panic escalate to a whole other level. What was wrong with her? Didn't she know that it was dangerous to let him become so important to her? Especially when the important people in her life always ended up leaving her, one way or the other…

'I am sorry you have been so sick in the mornings, Bliss,' Sandrine started to say. 'But don't worry, it will most probably subside in around five or six weeks or so. In the meantime I suggest you keep to a good, fresh diet and get lots of rest. I will give you a very good homeopathic remedy to help ease the discomfort a little. The instructions for taking them are on the label.' She placed a little coffee-coloured tube on the table filled with small white tablets. 'Other than that, I have to say you are in very good shape and should be able to look forward to a healthy and happy pregnancy.'

'Thank God!' Dante didn't think twice about reaching for Bliss's small hand and capturing it in his own. He curled his long bronzed fingers around hers and breathed an audible sigh of relief. Bliss herself suddenly found she was hardly capable of breathing at all. Was this what it might feel like to be loved and cherished? To have someone who cared for you demonstrate that your well-being was paramount? The thought planted itself in her mind before she could stop it and then cold reality hit like ice water as it occurred to her that Dante was only thinking of the baby's welfare and not hers. Pulling her hand free, Bliss tried not to glance at the genuine surprise crossing his face.

'Having said that, my dear, I do have a prescription to offer you, and that is that you let your wonderful husband-to-be take you home to Italy for a holiday. Isabella will be in seventh heaven fussing around her prospective daughter-in-law and you will get a much-needed rest, Bliss. Come back and see me after the wedding, yes?'

Finding herself nodding because in the face of Sandrine Lantain's sunny, confident smile she thought it rude to do otherwise, Bliss got to her feet, then tried to quell her jealousy as Dante kissed the obstetrician on both cheeks and bid her goodbye. When they were outside again, the dignified London street bathed in untypical sunshine, Dante paused for a moment to tilt Bliss's still-defiant chin towards him. Glancing into the surprise reflected in her beautiful violet eyes, he felt something warm and emphatic settle deep inside him that confirmed he was absolutely right to dictate what he was about to dictate—even though she clearly resented his taking over her life.

'Sandrine is right,' he announced, his words measured and precise. 'You *do* need a holiday. After we have arranged our marriage this afternoon at the register office, I am booking us on a flight to Milan. My parents have a villa in the countryside in Varese and I think it will be the perfect place for you to relax, as well as a good opportunity to meet them. If we are too late tonight to drive to the villa, then we will stay at my apartment in the city and make the drive tomorrow morning to Varese. I think you should know right now that I will not be taking no for an answer.'

Bliss felt a shiver run through her at the idea of travelling to Italy with Dante to meet his parents, and her inclination to argue died away like morning mist dispersing to let the sun shine through. Why shouldn't she enjoy a short break away from her day-to-day concerns? Dante was right. He and his doctor friend were both right. Opportunities for going on holiday had always been few and far between and, in truth, with all that had happened, she was in desperate need of one. Overriding her indignation that he seemed to be organising her life with or without her consent, Bliss feebly tried for a smile to acknowledge her agreement. But with Dante's hand caressing her shoulder and his seductive male heat infiltrating her blood, making her feel as heady as if she'd been drinking wine, she couldn't swear that she managed to pull the gesture off.

The effusive Italian voice on the radio drifted in and out of Bliss's consciousness as they drove through the night, Dante's confident, masterful manoeuvring of the luxurious Alfa Romeo car making their journey as smooth and as comfortable as flowing silk on the moonlit Italian roads. It seemed they were making the journey to Varese tonight after all and Bliss had tried to stem the wave of apprehension that flowed over her at this information, fear kicking in like a powerful narcotic in case her introduction to Dante's parents did not go well. How would they receive a girl they had never met before, who had appeared out of nowhere? What if they'd already had some nice little rich girl all lined up for their precious eldest son and were angry that Bliss had fallen pregnant with Dante's baby and ruined their hoped-for plans? As her anxious thoughts tumbled over one another, finally forcing her to open her eyes and make her shift in her seat, Dante glanced across at her, the concern in his eyes showing plainly for a second beneath the bright glare of a passing car's headlamps. 'What is wrong? You are feeling unwell, perhaps? I can stop the car if you need me to.'

Reaching for the bottle of water she'd put down by her feet, Bliss shook her head. 'I just needed a drink, that's all. Would you like some?' She took a swig and wiped her mouth with the back of her hand.

Per amor del cielo! How was it possible that she made the most simple gesture seem as though she were deliberately provoking him? Dante concentrated all his efforts to try and ignore the heat that throbbed fiercely through his veins like a rich, full-bodied Chianti, but it wasn't easy. Not when Bliss Maguire had the lushest, most ripely seductive mouth he had personally ever encountered. It was becoming more and more difficult for him to focus solely on her comfort and welfare when his own—perhaps more base—needs begged to be sated. With her dark hair tousled from sleep and travelling, her enormous lavender eyes regarding him sleepily and the moisture from the water she'd just imbibed glistening like dew on her mouth, just looking at her was the sweetest torture a tormentor could devise. Deliberately forcing himself to concentrate on the grey strip that curved narrowly round a hillside in front of him, Dante tried not to think about having her strip down to her skin and sharing his bed tonight. Because if he had any say in the matter at all, that was just how he intended it was going to be.

'Another hour and we should be there. No doubt Isabella will be waiting up to greet us.'

'Isabella? You mean your mother?'

'*Sì*. My mother.' Unable to stop himself from smiling at the thought of the woman who had raised him, Dante stole another glance at Bliss. 'She told me she cannot wait until tomorrow morning to meet you. My *papà*, on the other hand, has to go to bed early since his illness.'

Dante had told her on the flight out that his father Antonio was suffering from heart disease. Bliss had not missed the flash of fear in his troubled green eyes when he'd confided this information and her heart had hurt to imagine the pain this must cause him.

'Dante, you haven't told me how it will be. I mean, what must your parents think of you bringing a strange woman back home with you from England? Not to mention the fact that I'm pregnant.'

'*Sì*. Pregnant with my *bambino*.' His gaze was quick to seek out her still-flat stomach beneath her long linen skirt, hotly possessive and proud that this beautiful woman and her expected baby were both his. His bronzed fingers curved tightly round the leather steering wheel. 'You want to know how it will be, *cara*? They are happy that they are going to meet the beautiful girl who is to be their new daughter-in-law. My family have been wanting my marriage for years and now they are going to get what they wish for.'

'And they won't mind that I am not Italian, like you?'

Her innocent question caused such a spasm of shocked surprise inside his chest that Dante's jaw suddenly clenched hard as if to ward off unwanted, familiar feelings of somehow being a usurper in his own family. An outsider... He wanted to reveal to Bliss the secret he had not shared with her yet—that he had more in common with her own ancestry than she suspected. But part of him did not want to betray his father's past pain and, if he was honest, neither did he want to reveal his own. Now was not the time to tell Bliss that he was the result of Antonio's love affair. She had enough to contend with, with the prospect of meeting her new family. And besides, his own story might only add to her fears of not being accepted. Dante could appreciate her trepidation, but if his recent telephone conversation with Isabella had been any true indication of his parents' feelings, their happiness and enthusiasm at the announcement of his marriage would soon sweep away any reservations Bliss might be harbouring.

'No. They do not mind that you are not Italian. I can guarantee you that, at least.'

'Dante! *Mio figlio più amato!* How wonderful to see you.'

As Dante was enveloped in the waiting arms of his mother, Isabella, he couldn't deny the spurt of warmth that flooded his insides at her words. 'My most beloved son,' she'd called him, and no matter how many times she said it, it still had the power to unravel him a little emotionally. As he regarded the fragrant stucco porch scented heavily with flowering jasmine and his mother's small, rotund figure back-lit by the pool of light flowing out from the large rectangular hall inside, Dante couldn't deny the hope in his heart that this time he could lay his doubts to rest and truly be glad to be back home. That this time he would really feel accepted, with no distrust in his mind that he was not as loved or well thought of as Stefano and Tatiana. Perhaps the advent of the pretty, yet reserved woman by his side, soon to be his wife and the mother of his child, would help herald a new dawn of peace in his heart?

'*Mamma.* You should not have waited up so late, you look tired.' He kissed Isabella on both cheeks, his hand lingering a little on her shoulder as she smilingly waved him away to fix her gaze on the so-far-silent Bliss.

'Welcome, daughter. Come here into the light so that I can see you.'

Every muscle in her body clenched tight with apprehension, Bliss moved to Dante's side, comforted when he briefly grazed her fingers with his own as if to reassure her that everything was going to be all right. Her first impression of Isabella di Andrea was that the woman, though small and full figured, had the most beautifully arresting face, with sparkling eyes the same riveting blue as Tatiana's, curly chestnut hair and the smile of a proud *mamma* whose children and family were the very soul of her being. Immediately the tension in Bliss's body started to ease. It touched her that Isabella had called her 'daughter'. The woman didn't yet know her, yet she had welcomed her with an endearment that immediately told Bliss that she was more than willing to take her into her heart because she was marrying her precious son.

'I am very pleased to meet you, Mrs di Andrea.'

'Ay, ay, ay! I am *Mamma, sì*? And you are now my new daughter along with Tatiana and Monica—Stefano's wife.' Without further preamble, Isabella pulled Bliss's slender body against hers, then, setting her slightly apart, delivered two resounding kisses, one on each cheek. 'My son was right. He said you were *molto bella* and I see he did not tell a lie. But I must not keep you standing out here all night. When you are with child it is important to rest as much as possible in the first few months. Come in and I will show you to your room and bring you something warm to drink before you go to bed. In the morning you will meet my husband, Antonio, and then we can breakfast together and talk about the wedding, no?'

Bliss stole a very surreptitious glance at Dante and found him looking back at her with an expression that made her heart race. It was a possessive, almost predatory look that told her he had every intention of sharing her bed tonight and she'd better get used to the idea because under no circumstances was he going to be persuaded differently. Following a smiling Isabella inside the villa, Bliss almost missed the small raised step inside the porch because her blood was racing so hotly with anticipation through her veins.

Their large double bedroom had stone-flagged floors, frescos decorating the walls and antique furniture that was exquisite—including a large four-poster bed with flowing, damask rose drapes. Although she was almost painfully tired, Bliss's hungry eyes never wearied of gazing at beauty and so, while Dante busied himself bringing their cases in from the car, she took off the short linen jacket she'd worn over her shirt and walked around the room examining everything. Stopping at a silver filigree framed photograph of Dante with an older well-dressed man with very white teeth and silver hair smiling beside him, she surmised that this must be Antonio, Dante's father. As well as being extremely attractive with a very definite twinkle in his eye, his features suggested warmth and friendliness in abundance and Bliss couldn't help but feel reassured, and not quite so daunted any more at the prospect of meeting him tomorrow.

'*Mamma* is making you a drink. I said hot milk would be okay?'

Her attention was diverted as Dante entered the room

carrying both their suitcases, and she noted that he too had removed his jacket. As he put down the cases and shut the door behind him her pulse skittered nervously at the sight of him, because the man seemed to provoke such a groundswell of passion inside her breast that she almost felt light-headed. And travelling had clearly not taken its toll on him in the way that it had on Bliss. Her hair and clothes were mussed, her make-up non-existent and she was in dire need of a bath or a shower. In contrast, one could have been forgiven for thinking that Dante had just returned from a casual afternoon stroll round some of the fashion hot spots of Milan.

'Hot milk is fine, thanks, but I didn't want her to go to any trouble.'

'If you knew Isabella, you would know that she loves to fuss around her children.' As he paused to study her, his hands either side of his lean, tight hips in his stylish black jeans, Dante's examination of her was unnervingly intense. There was a definite tension about him that Bliss couldn't fail to detect immediately and it put her on her guard. She wet her lips slightly with her tongue. 'But I'm not one of her children, Dante, and she has only just met me.'

'Even so. You will have to get used to her wanting to mother you…especially now that she knows you are expecting her newest grandchild.' In a couple of strides he stood before her, his gaze touching her everywhere as if there wasn't a place on her face or body that he was willing to overlook. In fact, he was devouring her with those scintillating green eyes of his, so hotly that in response Bliss could only stand there and stare at him, feeling as though some invisible mystical power held her willing captive. 'Why are you l-looking at me like that?' she stammered out.

'You are not too tired from the journey?'

'Why do you want to know?' Her voice was a hushed whisper, her senses imprisoned by the rapaciously carnal glances Dante was giving her, feeling as if she'd been hooked up to some kind of honey drip that was slowing everything down and heating everything up all at the same time.

'Why do you think I want to know…huh?' Those irresistible fingers of his slid behind her neck and the pad of his thumb stroked back and forth across the sensitive skin on her throat in a very deliberate sensual foray. Leaning into his touch, Bliss couldn't prevent the gasp of pleasure that emanated from her lips, yet she couldn't deny the little niggle of disquiet inside her that refused to be stemmed either. 'Is this…is this the room you normally stay in when you come home to your parents' house?' she asked softly.

'Yes, it is. Why do you ask?'

'Well…do you normally bring your girlfriends home with you when you come to stay?'

The dawn of understanding stealing into his fascinating green eyes, Dante stopped stroking Bliss's throat and moved his hand down to rest it on her shoulder. There was the tiniest lift at the edges of his mouth, but Bliss couldn't have said whether the intriguing little gesture was meant to be a smile or not. 'I will tell you the truth, Bliss. I have never brought a girlfriend home to stay here with me. Always before we have stayed at my apartment in Milan.'

Trying to ignore the painful idea that he'd had any other girlfriends at all, let alone entertained them in his apartment, Bliss frowned. 'And your parents don't mind that we are sharing a room together before we are married?' There, she'd said it, hot, embarrassed colour pouring into her cheeks the moment the words were out.

Dante could not fail to be impressed by the fact that Bliss should take his parents' feelings into consideration. Impressed, but still enormously frustrated because how could he in all conscience argue if she were to suggest it was perhaps best if they didn't share a room? Certainly Isabella would secretly applaud Bliss's unexpected show of respect. 'Clearly they do not mind, or *Mamma* would not have told me to put our cases in the same room, *innamorata*. Besides...' his gaze flicked downwards across her slim abdomen in her long black linen skirt '...it is a little late in the day to be so modest, is it not?'

His candid comment was not what she'd wanted to hear and, painfully disconcerted, Bliss raised her chin in a bid to hold onto her dignity. 'Late in the day or not, Dante, I think we should wait until after we are married to share a room in your parents' house. Don't you agree?'

A visible muscle throbbing in the side of one tanned, perfectly sculpted cheek, Dante scowled and strode angrily to the other side of the room, as if he could hardly believe the disappointing turn events had suddenly taken. 'You are doing this to torment me, are you not?' he burst out.

Bliss almost wanted to laugh at the pure frustration in his eyes, but she couldn't. Because if he was frustrated at them not being together in the most intimate way, she was wondering how she was supposed to spend the night in that big, gorgeous bed alone without every bit of possible sleep being disrupted by tormenting thoughts of having Dante make love to her, wildly and without restraint.

CHAPTER TEN

STANDING on the white veranda that lined the upper floor of the villa next morning, with miles and miles of verdant green forest in the distance, Bliss breathed deeply of the jasmine-scented summer air with a newly stirring, fragile sense of hope in her heart. Dante had been frustrated and angry when she had suggested they did not share a room in deference to his parents, yet he had still wished her a good night's rest and told her not to worry about rising early the next morning. Now as she admired the view, the sounds of breakfast being prepared in the background with Isabella's melodic Italian peppering the air, Bliss hoped Dante had forgiven her for not allowing him to share her bed. Although she had initially tossed and turned due to her own undeniable frustration, eventually sheer fatigue had caught up with her and she had slept the sleep of the truly innocent. Even succumbing to another bout of morning sickness had not encroached upon her satisfaction at that.

'Buona mattina.'

He took her by surprise, coming up behind her and sliding his hands down her bare arms in her white sleeveless blouse. Inevitably, Bliss's heartbeat went wild at the sensation of his warm, tantalising flesh against hers. He smelt so good, too, fresh and clean and as sexy and promising as a Mediterranean summer.

'Good morning.'

'I think this is my favourite spot.'

'I don't blame you, the view is amazing.'

'I meant *this* spot.' To Bliss's shock, Dante pressed his lips against the curve where her shoulder joined her neck and his heat and touch combined were like a firebrand. How was she expected to withstand such pleasure almost beyond imagining?

'I missed not having you in my bed last night.' His mouth moved up with maddening slowness to her ear and kissed that too. Inside her blouse, Bliss's breasts grew heavy and achy with desire and she yearned to experience his touch again there too.

'Dante…your parents might see.' She twisted round so that she was facing him, and her breath was all but stolen from her lungs at the sight of the sexy, slumberous smile playing about his taunting lips.

'What will they see?' he asked carelessly. 'Their son showing his appreciation for the beautiful woman he is going to marry?'

'You don't have to marry me, Dante.' Unable to prevent her fears from stealing her joy of the moment, Bliss tried to avoid his searching gaze. She might be going to have his child, but she still could not understand why he seemed so eager…*happy* almost, at the idea of marrying her. How could she possibly compare to all the truly beautiful girls that must gaze at Dante and sigh for his attention? She was a veritable nobody…an ex-shop assistant who hadn't had a clue what she wanted to do with the rest of her life until Dante had inadvertently walked into it. While, in contrast, he was everything. And didn't he deserve to be in love with the woman he married? Not be forced to wed her just because she was expecting his child?

'What do you mean, I don't have to marry you?' He stepped back a little, his expression wary.

'I know things seem pretty imperative…because of the

baby and everything. But surely people should marry because they love each other. Not just out of necessity.' As soon as the words were out of her mouth Bliss regretted her unguarded moment. It was almost like bearing her soul to confess such a loaded opinion—as if she secretly did believe in falling in love and happy ever after, when she knew the opposite to be true. Her skin prickling with discomfort because Dante appeared in no hurry to comment one way or the other, Bliss was about to turn away when his words stopped her in her tracks.

'I think I will come to care for you a great deal, Bliss, if that is what you are worrying about. But we have to give our marriage time. I will be a good husband, I think. You and our child will not want for anything. And you will not lack passion in your life, I promise you. I will be a faithful and attentive lover.'

His eyes visibly darkened like a Connemara sky when the sun set in the west, and Bliss didn't doubt he meant every word. The very air between them when they were together was ignitable. But still a small part of her heart seemed to curl up and die at the absence of the word 'love' in his reply.

'And you will not feel that something is…that something is missing, Dante?' she asked quietly, her violet eyes glistening in her small heart-shaped face.

'*Buongiorno,* Bliss! I have waited a long time for this moment and I will not wait a moment longer!'

Swallowing down her hurt, Bliss nevertheless found a smile for the tall, imposing man in his rolled-up shirtsleeves walking slowly but determinedly towards her with the use of a cane. Feeling herself enveloped in what she could only describe as a huge bear hug, she glanced at Dante past his father's shoulder and was gratified at least to find that he was smiling too.

'You must be Antonio? Dante's father. I've been so looking forward to meeting you too.'

Antonio grinned from ear to ear at her polite but warm greeting. As he turned towards his son it would have been hard to find a more happy man on earth right then by the delight on his face.

'She is charming, Dante, just charming! My Ana told me I would like her and she was right.' Returning his attention to Bliss, Antonio sagely nodded his silver-grey head, something poignant and deeply stirring in his dark brown eyes as his gaze surveyed her. 'I make up my mind very quickly about people, Bliss Maguire—and already I know that you are going to make my beloved son the best wife. Yes...I *know* that.'

'*Papà* is happier than I have seen him for a long time, my son.' Arranging some fruit in a bowl on the raffia table, Isabella di Andrea paused for a long moment to rest her gaze on Dante's tall, restless figure as he paced slowly from one end of the long wraparound veranda to the other. With a mother's concern, she knew he had a lot on his mind right then, and most of it was no doubt concerning the young woman that was soon to be his wife.

'You know that your happiness means everything to him?'

'Does it?' Wishing he could push away the inevitable onrush of hurt that arose inside his chest at the familiar doubts that beset him, Dante glanced at his mother, then quickly glanced away again.

Isabella looked stunned. 'You have to ask me that question, son? You must know your father worships the ground you walk upon. He always has!'

'You don't think that I am a disappointment to him?

A reminder of the fact that his parents rejected him because of my birth?'

Isabella's hands dropped to her sides. Behind the brilliant sapphire hue of her eyes, Dante could see that she was shocked.

'Where has this nonsense come from, Dante di Andrea? You know that you could not possibly be a disappointment to Antonio! And it was your *papà* who rejected his parents because they refused to countenance his relationship with Katherine, even when she was expecting his child. It is sad that they are gone, but Antonio does not regret breaking ties with them. They were bitter with him about Katherine to the end—they would not even acknowledge your existence. Your *papà* had to struggle to support you. Can you blame your father for doing what he did?'

'I do not blame *Papà*. Of course I don't!' Feeling emotion well up inside him and almost threaten to unbalance him, Dante gripped the white balustrade of the veranda and stared unseeingly out at the vista of chestnut trees that made up the forest in the distance. 'It was not his fault that I was different.'

'Different?' Now Isabella pulled out a chair and sat in it, her hands no longer busy with arranging fruit.

'I felt different,' Dante repeated, glancing only briefly across at the woman in the chair. 'Illegitimate. Not a member of the family. I was jealous of Stefano and Tatiana. I was on my own for a long time until *Papà* married you, and *Papà* was always working and did not have a lot of time for me. Then when you had my brother and sister your love for them was guaranteed because they were your natural children. Any falling out between the three of us, I blamed on myself because I was not of the same blood. An outsider. Every day I grew more and more aware that I was not the same as them. It made me work harder and harder to impress my father—to have his approval so that he would never regret having me.' His green eyes narrowing, Dante turned to face his mother. 'I wanted your unconditional love too, Isabella. I wanted you to be as proud of me as you are of Stefano and Tatiana.'

Without regard that she was not as young and as lithe as she used to be, Isabella fairly flew across the space separating them to pull Dante into her arms. Murmuring endearments over and over again as she stroked his hair and kissed his face, she did not once feel ashamed for crying. The mere existence of Dante's belief that he had never thought himself truly her son, or that she did not love him with the same passionate devotion as her other two children, almost had the ability to stop her heart from beating. 'You were my first *bambino*, Dante, and I loved you from the very first moment I saw you. So serious you were with your sad green eyes and wary looks! A mother's first child always holds a special place in her heart. My son, I would give up my life for you and would feel privileged to do so.'

'*Sì.*' His throat convulsing and unable to prevent the hot well of tears that filled his eyes, Dante clasped Isabella hard into his chest and held her. 'I would do the same for you, *Mamma.*'

Dozing in the sunshine, Bliss heard a movement behind her. When a large hand pressed comfortingly down upon her shoulder, she removed her sunglasses and sat up, startled to find Antonio di Andrea beaming down at her. He lowered himself into the white raffia chair next to her sun lounger, his smiling brown eyes not leaving her for a moment.

'You know what you have done for me, Bliss?'

Not knowing either what to say or what to expect next, Bliss stayed silent.

'You must forgive the cliché, but you have made an old man very, very happy. Of all my children, I have always worried about Dante the most. He is not like Stefano or Tatiana. When he has a problem he takes it inside himself; he does not share it with his family. With you as his wife, he will learn to share his worries and you will be a comfort and a support to him.'

Slipping her sunglasses back onto her nose, Bliss was inundated with an ache so strong, she had to take a minute to compose herself. What would Dante say if he knew that she had fallen in love with him and would gladly be his comfort and support in times of stress if he so wished it? Would he think twice about marrying her because he wouldn't want to disappoint her in that department himself? He'd told her that he would be a good husband, and that she wouldn't lack passion in her life, but what was passion without love in a relationship? It would be like a beautiful bloom left to die without being tended. Denied water and sustenance, it would eventually wither and turn to dust.

'Your son is a good man, Mr di Andrea.' What could she say to Dante's father but state the obvious? Another man would have run a mile at the knowledge that a woman he'd known only briefly was pregnant with his child, but Dante had not tried to escape his responsibilities.

'Please, call me Antonio. Do me this honour, *piccola*. I have just lost a precious son-in-law, but God is good because now I am to gain another beautiful daughter.'

'That's kind of you to say.'

Antonio's bushy eyebrows shot up to his hairline. 'You

will learn this about me, Bliss. I never say things I do not mean. And I do not forget that you also helped my beloved daughter in her hour of need. And now you are to give my son a child…that makes my heart glad too. I am not surprised that Dante should see you and immediately fall in love.'

She was glad of the dark shield of her sunglasses at that moment, as it took every ounce of courage she had in her for Bliss to hold back her tears. Dante *hadn't* fallen in love with her, as Antonio surmised, but right now she would not want to disappoint an already ill man with such a confession. He clearly thought the world of his son and if it brought him ease to believe that theirs was a love match, then who was Bliss to deny him that joy?

'*Papà.*' The subject of both their thoughts appeared through the patio doors, looking suntanned and gorgeous in a white shirt and tan trousers, his bronzed feet intriguingly bare. 'I am to inform you that your nurse says it is time for you to take your medication.'

Antonio's eyes twinkled with merriment as he glanced first at Bliss, then his son. 'She is a tyrant, that one. Your *mamma* must have hired her from the military, make no mistake!'

Bliss automatically left her lounger to help him get back onto his feet as he briefly struggled to right himself and get hold of his walking cane. But Dante was just as swift, his hand glancing against hers as his arm came around his father's ample waist and helped him get his bearings.

'Military or not, she is here for your benefit, *Papà*, and you must heed her advice, *sì*?'

'Okay, okay! You don't have to fuss around me like I am a two-year-old, eh? Stay here with your lovely young woman and enjoy your free time together before *Mamma* descends on you both again with talk of your wedding! And I hope that you have told Bliss that we have friends and relatives coming over this afternoon to meet her? Do not be alarmed, Bliss, they are all good people and only want to share in our joy that our son is getting married.'

But Bliss did feel alarmed. Suddenly this coming marriage of theirs was becoming too real and too close for comfort. How could she possibly back out of it when everyone was being told that it was going to happen? More to the point—how could she disappoint Isabella and Antonio when they had opened their arms to her unquestioningly and been so kind?

Catching the fleeting panic in her eyes, Dante dipped his head in a brief nod, as if to say, We will talk.

When he had seen her sitting there out on the veranda conversing with his father, Dante had been unable to deny the sense of pleasure the sight had given him. She was looking exquisitely beautiful in a white sun-top with thin shoestring straps and a white antique-lace skirt, her pretty feet bare and her dark hair softly caressing the back of her neck, and he had let the inevitable heat the sight of her stirred roll over him. Combined with the already fierce heat of the nearly noonday sun beating down on the veranda, it had made him think of—and more urgently, *want*—only one thing. Seeing his father safely inside into the care of his nurse, Dante did not linger in his return to the veranda.

'Perhaps you should come inside? It is very hot sitting out here and I do not want you to burn.'

Reaching for her sunscreen, Bliss twisted off the cap and threw him a brief smile behind her glasses. 'I'm okay. I've got my protection. You can't deny me the enjoyment of some sun after the weather we usually have to endure at home.'

Her words transfixed him. Right now he did not want to deny her a single thing. If she were to ask him for the largest, most precious, most desired jewel in the world, he would do his best to get it for her. Once again the realisation that she carried his child inside her womb stirred deeply powerful feelings of possession and protection inside him, making him wish their wedding were today and not in nearly two weeks' time. 'If you're going to insist on staying out here a little while longer then at least let me make sure you will not burn.'

Before Bliss realised what he intended, he pulled up the raffia chair his father had just vacated and sat in it, then took the tube of sunscreen out of her hand. 'Pull down your straps,' he ordered, his voice barely able to maintain its equilibrium at the sight of her unblemished, silky skin.

Her hand trembled as she undertook what should have been a perfectly easy, straightforward request and she just thanked her lucky stars that she hadn't been foolish enough to sit out here in her swimsuit, which was what she had originally considered when she had realised how warm it was. At least there was not too much bare skin on show for her to worry about. But as Dante's beautiful hands began to rub cream into first one shoulder, then the other, Bliss had to shut her eyes to absorb the tiny explosions of exquisitely sensual sensation that he triggered all over her body. She squirmed with the need to let him touch her all over. She even had to squeeze her thighs together to prevent them from naturally relaxing and inviting his attention to that secret place at their apex. There was no doubt about it, Dante di Andrea had a touch that was intoxicating. Just one brief glance of his flesh against hers could make Bliss come undone. He might be just rubbing sunscreen into a perfectly respectable area of skin, but, as far as Bliss was concerned, he could just as well be making love to her out here in the open. The thought sent a fresh throb of need flooding through her bloodstream because suddenly the very idea of doing just that was so powerful that she almost told him out loud what was in her mind and to hell with the consequences. At the last moment, she bit down hard on her lip to prevent herself from saying anything.

All the moisture in Dante's mouth seemed to evaporate when he saw her nipples clearly harden inside the thin material of her sun-top. Then, before Bliss could protest, he started to sensuously rub cream into the exposed area just above her breasts, his fingers every so often dipping below the square neckline of her top to reach underneath and get closer and closer to that part of her body that he longed to caress. Not just with his fingers, but with his lips and his tongue and his teeth. *Santo cielo!* If there was an exercise in sheer, sensual torture, then this must surely be it. Did the woman want to drive him out of his mind, letting him do something as provocative as massage sun cream into her skin? He swore. Out loud. Even though the curse had been in his native Italian, he knew that Bliss could not fail to recognise that it was no line of poetry.

'What's wrong?' Perturbed, she hastily pushed back the shoestring straps of her top into place and twisted round to look at Dante.

'I want to take you somewhere.'

If the fierce noonday heat was making her skin sizzle, then Dante's hot, hungry gaze was all but making her burst into flames.

'Where?' Her voice was a mere husk of its former self in response.

'Somewhere that we can be alone.'

*   *   *

He spread out the blanket beneath the grove of trees and, sheltered by the thick leafy foliage they provided, he urged Bliss to the ground with him, holding her gaze as intently as only a man pushed to the limits of his desire could.

'You may not feel comfortable with us sharing a room in my parents' house, but out here we can be free, no?'

Making no protest when he urged her urgently into his arms, Bliss knew her will was already banished to some far-off country when it came to resisting Dante. She had no will around him—at least not one that would help her stay this side of sensible.

He massaged her silky lower lip with his finger, then trailed the same finger down onto her chin and lower, much lower, until it came to rest between the cleft of her breasts inside her top. A small pearl of perspiration slid down between her cleavage and Dante captured it with his finger, using it to make tantalising circles on her skin. Bliss sucked in her breath until it all but squeezed her lungs to bursting point, such was the tension and trembling that his action elicited. Already her nipples had puckered to a point almost past bearing and damp heat spread up the front of her thighs into her most feminine core like warm waves lapping onto a shore.

'Do you know what I went through last night when I couldn't touch you as I wanted?' He breathed the taunting question next to her throat as his hand drifted ever downwards and palmed the fullness of her breast. As she helplessly surged against him her body came into full contact with his chest, where he had already undone the buttons of his shirt. Coming into intimate relations with flesh and bone that had the devastating tenacity of steel yet was silkily smooth and tantalisingly warm beneath her fingers, Bliss wondered how she'd ever imagined she could do without most things the male of the species had to offer. But that was before she'd met Dante. Right now the pleasure he was wreaking throughout her body was so intense that the idea of living without it was not to be borne.

But before she could further contemplate what the absence of his touch might mean in her life, Dante cupped her face and brought his mouth down onto her lips in a searing, uncompromising kiss that washed away all thought as thoroughly as a drenching rain swept away sand. His lips and tongue commanding the pace, he coaxed and teased, demanded then retreated, turning up the pleasure as only a man well schooled in the art of lovemaking knew how to do. Before she knew it, Bliss was transported to a world so exquisitely sensual that she easily forgot every single concern or worry she'd ever had and willingly yielded to the compelling enchantment that was woven around her. Beneath Dante's devastating touch her limbs turned fluid and boneless and she readily capitulated to his teasing regime, letting her softly rasping breath fan across his face before another hungry, devastating kiss could capture the breath that came directly after.

Between a break in the lofty chestnut boughs above them, the sun filtered through in a laser beam of heat, lazily drifting across Bliss's back as Dante lay down on the blanket and eased her against his hips. Pushing her white lace skirt up to the top of her smooth, slender thighs, he worked his fingers into her skin in a provocative massage, easing them ever upwards towards the destination that he so clearly sought. Already drenched with heat and longing, Bliss closed her eyes on a quivering little groan as he slid his finger inside her, rubbing against her most tender core until she could swear she literally saw stars as throb after throb of exquisite sensory pleasure washed over her, as if she were lying naked on a bed of golden sand beneath a spicy Caribbean sun. Time stopped. She felt herself connected to everything around her, the trees, the air and most especially the earth upon which she and her lover lay, and nothing in Bliss's life had ever felt so absolutely right and good. Tears of pleasure and gratitude swam in the vibrant sea of her violet eyes. But before she could recover her breath, Dante was eagerly helping her part company with her white silk panties, then settling her urgently against him as he unzipped his trousers and eased the full length of his erection deeply inside her. Looking down at him as she was once again deluged in a fountain of sensory pleasure unimagined, Bliss could see that his eyes had turned as hot and as vivid as molten emerald. Bending her head to kiss him, she was taken aback by the almost violent clash of lips, tongue and teeth as his mouth claimed fierce ownership of hers, the erotically sensuous scent of his skin mingling with the scent of her own as he drove himself deeper inside her.

He cried out just as Bliss climaxed only seconds before him, his richly vibrant male voice echoing around her as his hips pumped against the softer, silkier texture of her smooth inner thighs. Greedily his hands guided her pelvis passionately upon his sex as though he wanted to extract every single drop of satisfaction and enjoyment she had to give and would not be happy with anything less.

'How am I supposed to think about anything else today after you have almost made me lose my mind with desire for you?' His face, relaxed of all tension, was so heart-rendingly handsome, almost boyish, that Bliss knew a moment of delirious joy. She almost couldn't speak for the happiness pouring through her. Perhaps everything was going to be all right after all? When they were together like this she could almost believe anything were possible. Unwilling to break the profound connection she had found in his arms, she boldly cupped his face with her hands and smiled down into his hypnotic, long-lashed eyes with all the confidence of a woman who knew without doubt just how much pleasure she had given her man.

'Who says we have to think, Dante? Can't we just feel?'

'*Si, carina.*' His voice growing husky, Dante reached for the shoestring straps of Bliss's top and pulled them firmly down her arms so that the whole garment went with them and her beautiful breasts were fully exposed to his hotly possessive glance as the sun continued to shine through the trees. 'I think that is a very good suggestion. *Bellissima* Bliss. I think you have made me your slave for life. Perhaps we should stay here for the rest of the day and just "feel", hmm?' His hands cupped her breasts as he said this and squeezed them. Sensing him hardening beneath her, Bliss could not suppress the soft, almost desperate moan that escaped her.

'We—we can't just stay here, Dante. Your family is expecting guests this afternoon, remember?' Her brow furrowing with regret, Bliss endeavoured to move, feeling suddenly guilty, worrying about what Dante's family would think should they return to the villa late and obviously flushed with the results of their lovemaking. But she stared at Dante open-mouthed in shock as he caught her wrists and held her, such a look of lascivious lust in his eyes that Bliss momentarily lost the power of speech. Rolling her expertly over onto her back, he smiled down at her with unconcealed primeval satisfaction. 'The guests can wait. Right now *il Presidente* himself can wait until I have sated myself with your body.'

CHAPTER ELEVEN

SIPPING from a glass of fruit punch, Bliss surreptitiously glanced around at the well-dressed gathering of guests milling around the *terrazzo*, her outwardly calm expression belying the deep-seated anxiety that was rolling through her inside. She didn't fit in here, nor did she belong. With their relaxed, sometimes passionately charged voices permeating the warm summer air, along with the tinkle of glasses and the scrape of cutlery against Isabella's exquisite crockery, the people at the party seemed like a breed apart to Bliss. And of course they *were*. Place her in a line-up with them and ask someone to pick the odd one out, and she didn't doubt that she would be the first choice. The impressive line-up of cars on the gravel drive also highlighted the colossal differences in their lifestyles. Along with at least three fabulous Ferraris, there was also one Rolls Royce and a Lamborghini, as well as several other expensive vehicles.

What would Isabella's fabulously wealthy party guests think when they discovered that Dante's wife-to-be was an ex-shop assistant and one without any kind of connections—never mind wealthy—at all? She didn't want to shame Dante with her past. Didn't want him to have to deal with questions like, 'Who is her family? What do they do for a living?' and then see the quietly disappointed, even disapproving looks that crept into the questioners' eyes when they found out the answers. She had felt so certain that everything was going to be all right when she and Dante had been alone together under the chestnut trees earlier, but now… Now doubt would not leave her alone.

'I cannot believe my cousin has left you standing here all on your own. I have been watching you for some time now, expecting his return, but, as he has not appeared, I feel it is only right I should come and introduce myself. I am Alessandro Visconti and, as I know everyone else here, I take it you must be the beautiful girl who has finally captured his heart?'

The man who made his presence felt was young, about twenty-three or four, black-haired and good-looking, and—it went without saying—beautifully dressed. A waft of spicy but understated cologne with a probably ludicrous price tag floated up on the warm air to her nostrils as Bliss automatically accepted his relaxed handshake, inwardly praying that she wouldn't let her own composure slip and appear nervous.

'I'm Bliss Maguire.' *And I haven't captured Dante's heart—I've merely made him feel obliged to marry me because I'm pregnant.*

Alessandro's smiling black eyes sauntered casually and a little boldly up and down her figure in the simple blue summer dress she wore, then returned to smile even more widely into her uncertain gaze. 'Dante is a lucky man. A very *lucky* man, if you do not mind me saying so.'

Why was a simple telephone call taking so long? Bliss fretted silently. Dante had been gone at least fifteen minutes or more. She'd been introduced to practically everyone apart from this Alessandro Visconti, and, with Antonio going inside to take his medicine and Isabella accompanying her husband, there had been nothing for it but for Bliss to stand here on her own feeling ridiculously lonely and conspicuous. And, after their erotic little adventure beneath the chestnut trees earlier, Bliss was missing her husband-to-be as she would miss one of her own limbs were she to be separated from it. Somehow, over the course of just a few days, he had begun to mean everything to her and that gave Dante a power over her that was frankly terrifying to a girl who'd sworn she'd never fall in love, never mind get married.

'So…do you work in the hotel business too, Alessandro?' Taking a quick sip of her refreshing drink, Bliss told herself it shouldn't be so hard to make small talk with Dante's engaging cousin. With a little lift of his blue-black brows, he grinned unashamedly.

'No. I am what you might call the black sheep of the family. I spend my family's money like there is no to-morrow and, even worse, I travel around the casinos of the world gambling.'

'And do you ever win when you gamble?' Bliss asked interestedly, finding her attention unexpectedly captured by Alessandro's unabashed honesty.

'Sometimes.' He shrugged. 'And when I do I give it all to charity…of course. So perhaps I shouldn't feel so guilty about squandering the family fortune, eh?'

She had to laugh at that. It was the first easy moment she had enjoyed all day and Dante's young cousin laughed right along with her.

'What's so funny?'

Taking them both by surprise, Dante's tall, imperious figure suddenly appeared beside them, the sombre expression on his handsome face silently castigating them both.

'I was just telling your beautiful wife-to-be that I am the family rogue, Dante. No doubt you will agree with me?'

'It is indeed a role you play to the hilt without any remorse, Alessandro.' Making no attempt to hide the censure in his tone, Dante remained unsmiling, his expression disapproving. Feeling strangely disappointed that he should not find the slightest bit of charm in his cousin's engaging manner, Bliss was sufficiently moved to jump to the younger man's defence.

'We are none of us perfect, Dante. Wouldn't you agree?'

He clearly didn't agree at all, Bliss saw with a shiver skating down her spine. The same eyes that had regarded her so ardently only just a very short while ago under the chestnut trees were now as cold and spectacularly aloof as a glacier.

'I think it is time you went inside out of the sun, Bliss. I will accompany you.'

'But I don't want to—'

Silencing her protest with an even icier glance, Dante positioned his hand firmly beneath her elbow and led her away from the gathering on the *terrazzo*, leaving Alessandro staring after them.

In her bedroom, Bliss shook off Dante's hold on her arm, put down her drink and faced him furiously. 'What was all that about? It was very rude of you to walk away from your cousin like that!'

'Do not presume to speak to me as if you know what you are talking about!' With his brows drawing together like black clouds blocking out the sun, Dante glared at Bliss with such fury that it made her own anger seem completely impotent in comparison.

'Alessandro is a young jerk! He has almost caused his mother a breakdown with his bad behaviour, not to mention squandering a large proportion of the family's money on gambling and women! For this he has no remorse, no shame, and yet every time he comes home to his poor, tormented mother he is forgiven, and she believes him when he promises he will not behave in such a disrespectful way again.'

'You sound as though you resent that.'

Her astute comment silenced the words that were on the tip of Dante's tongue. Scraping his fingers through his hair, he turned away briefly to regain control of his temper and his composure. Merciful Father, he *did* resent it! Alessandro could behave as badly as he liked and yet he was loved and adored unconditionally by both his parents. In fact he played the role of 'Italian Playboy' to the hilt and was admired for it because his blood seemed to give him the right. And now Bliss—the woman Dante had pledged himself to—appeared to be as enchanted by his infamous cousin as everyone else! A little muscle throbbed in the side of his temple, giving testament to the white-hot rage that was searing his blood.

'Your interest in my cousin is not welcome,' he ground out through gritted teeth. 'Do not forget that you belong to me now. You will not look at another man with desire and you will never leave me! Is that understood?'

His words shocked Bliss rigid. Did he really believe that she could possibly be attracted to someone like Alessandro over him? And after she had loved him this afternoon as she had loved no other? Hurt, anger and dismay almost brought tears to her eyes.

'Don't boss me around! You have no right to talk to me like I'm some kind of possession. I belong to no one but myself!'

In a flood of unstoppable Italian, Dante vented his spleen out loud. When he'd finished, there was a tense, silent pause as they stared at each other. He took a breath, then shook his head and examined Bliss's slender, hurt figure with regret.

'Perhaps I do,' he said, gravel-voiced, hardly trusting himself to stay level-headed and calm beneath the onslaught of emotion that was coursing through him.

'Do what?' Bliss asked resentfully, still smarting from the fury obviously directed at her.

'I *do* resent Alessandro,' Dante admitted, his jaw reddening a little.

Seeing the glint of an old hurt in his eyes, Bliss had to know the full extent of what was troubling him. Now and again she had sensed a certain insecurity in Dante that she could hardly believe was possible in such a devastatingly attractive and successful man and she was sensing it again now. Her own anger died a swift death when she considered that he might be carrying wounds that wouldn't heal. Especially when she remembered how his father had told her that his eldest son took his problems inside himself and did not share them with his family.

'What *is* it, Dante? Is it just your cousin you are so angry about, or is it something else?'

He walked over to the window where there was a fine view of the grove of chestnut trees in the distance and, closer to home, the family's guests making themselves comfortable on the *terrazzo* in the afternoon sunshine.

'I do not have the same mother as my sister and brother.' Swallowing across the dryness in his throat, he continued to stare out of the window. 'My real mother was Irish—just like your father, Bliss. Does that surprise you?' Turning his head, he didn't wait for an acknowledgement. 'Her name was Katherine O'Brien and my father fell deeply in love with her almost the moment he met her. When she became pregnant and my father wanted them to be married, his parents would neither give their approval nor their blessing to the union. Shortly after that my mother died. For six years my father brought me up on his own, struggling to get his business under way at the same time. I was left with my aunt during the day, and she—she disapproved of my mere existence. Life was very tough for my father until he met Isabella. And then, when Tatiana and Stefano came along, I was no longer *numero uno* in my father's eyes. Is that selfish of me to miss that? My family mean everything to me but…sometimes I have felt like an outsider because of my background. This is an old culture. Tradition is not easily put aside for more modern ways. *Comprende?*'

Bliss did understand. Dante worked so hard to make his family proud of him, somehow believing that he had to buy their acceptance—to prove what? That he was as worthy of love as his brother and sister? The very idea was preposterous! What he couldn't seem to see, and Bliss could, was that they absolutely adored him and would do so whether he was a rich entrepreneur or a plumber. She only had to remember the look of love in Tatiana's eyes every time she trained them on Dante and she had seen the same look—if not more intensely—in both Antonio's and Isabella's eyes too.

'You have no need to be jealous of your cousin, Dante. From what I have seen of your relations, there is no doubt in my mind that you are very much loved and admired. You must try to put aside your reservations about that and be grateful that you clearly have such a wonderful family. Think about it this way…' Moving across the room to join him, Bliss ventured to place her hand on his arm. Beneath her fingers there was a definite stiffening in the already taut muscles beneath the soft fabric of his shirt, but she didn't let it curtail what she wanted to say. 'Would you want our child to suffer in the same way you have just because he or she has mixed ancestry? What about little Renata as well? Her father was English, wasn't he? Yet Antonio spoke very highly of his son-in-law. He clearly didn't mind that Tatiana fell in love with a man who was not Italian.'

'My father is not to blame. He never made me feel different in any way, but my birth caused a rift between him and his parents that was never mended. My birth deprived Stefano and Tatiana of their paternal grandparents too. You must understand...' His green eyes blazed back at her with profound emotion. 'These things are not easy for me to talk about. I have never discussed the matter with anyone else before until today.' With Isabella and now with Bliss—the lavender-eyed temptress who was even now stirring his blood again just because he was casting his gaze over her alluring, lovely presence.

'But I will tell you one thing: our child will have everything. There will be no sense of shame that he doesn't belong. I swear it!' Fastening his fingers firmly round Bliss's upper arms, he impelled her towards him. 'And my parents will adore their new grandchild; I am certain of that.'

'If our baby has unconditional love, Dante, he will not have to worry about anything else,' Bliss said quietly, for once feeling brave enough to meet his piercing gaze head-on.

'Sì,' he replied, grazing his knuckles thoughtfully across her cheek. 'In this you are right.'

Dante had to go to Milan on business. That was what the phone call had been about. He told her he would be gone two or three days at most, then he would be back. In the meantime he commanded Bliss to rest as much as possible and let Isabella and the home help do as much as possible to help her enjoy her stay. He'd said goodbye with a brief kiss, a shutter coming down over his beautiful eyes when he studied Bliss, as if he regretted being so frank with her yesterday. It made her feel desperately sad that he still did not trust her sufficiently to let her get close. Yesterday, when Dante had revealed the truth about his parentage, her heart had lifted with hope because at last they had seemed to be making some headway getting to know each other. But now Bliss was miserable and unsure again about their future. How would they fare in such a marriage if they were both continually guarded about their feelings?

Hearing voices in the hallway, Bliss collected her magazine and was on her way out to the veranda to sit for a while and read when Isabella appeared with Alessandro Visconti beside her.

'You have a visitor, my dear. I do not entirely approve of my nephew, if I am honest, but he is young like you and may provide a little welcome company while I make a visit to the hospital with Antonio this afternoon for his check-up.'

Her surprised glance colliding with Alessandro's irrepressible grin, Bliss found she didn't have the heart to tell Isabella that she would rather be alone with her thoughts than have to make conversation with someone she hardly knew. But then everyone was being so kind, making sure her every need was taken care of, that it would surely seem churlish to refuse Alessandro's company.

'Fine,' she said, nodding her head a little. 'Thank you, Isabella…and I hope everything goes well at the hospital.'

There was a brief glimpse of anxiety in Isabella's vivid

blue eyes, but her determinedly warm smile quickly drew attention away from it.

'*Sì*. I too hope the news is good. I know Antonio is feeling so much better since you and Dante came home so I am sure your visit is doing him good. Don't stay out in the sun too long will you, *mia cara*? I will see you later. *Arrivederci*.'

'So... I have got you all to myself for the afternoon.' Following Bliss out onto the veranda, Alessandro stood and watched as she settled herself comfortably into the sun lounger, his bold glance gravitating to the toned, beautifully shaped legs revealed by the white denim shorts she wore.

'I wouldn't quite put it like that.' Suddenly getting a mental vision of Dante's disapproving frown, Bliss was quick to ensure that Alessandro did not have the upper hand for even a second. She might have been initially cross with Dante for his rudeness to and jealousy of his cousin, but now she couldn't help but believe that behind that charming and affable smile of Alessandro's lurked a slightly more mercenary streak. She would definitely have to keep her wits about her. 'Did you come to visit with your cousin?' she asked, placing her magazine on the small raffia table beside her.

He grimaced. 'I found myself at a loose end and came to pay my respects to my uncle, but I am not exactly flavour of the month with any of my family at the moment, and least of all with Dante. Forgive me for being so frank with you, Bliss, but he just has to snap his fingers and the women come running, yet he always behaves like the perfect gentleman. My mother always says, ''Why can you not be more like Dante?'' But it is not in me to be so good, I'm afraid.'

Walking across to the white balustrade of the veranda,

Alessandro tossed his head as if to say, Ah, well, that's life, then turned back to Bliss, his eyes suddenly seeming to light up.

'I should take you for a drive through the countryside in my new car. It is really my *papà's* car, but I know he will let me have it if I tell him I can't live without it.'

'Do you always get what you want, Alessandro?' Bliss asked with a frown, sure as she spoke that she already knew the answer. How different his privileged childhood must have been from her own.

'Yes, probably.' He shrugged his shoulders in his light blue shirt without a hint of regret. 'But then I am charming, am I not? And being charming is very attractive to people, no?'

'Charm will only get you so far, I think. After that there has to be something of a little more substance. People are not so easily fooled as you might think.'

'I can see why my cousin fell for you, Bliss. Apart from your beauty, you are also intelligent. Dante has said many times that there has to be more than physical attraction to keep his attention.'

But would she be able to keep her husband's attention in the months to come? If he could get any woman he wanted, what reason would he have for sticking with her—apart from the baby? He clearly didn't love her. Her throat ached so much she had trouble swallowing down her misery. She was in a beautiful place surrounded by breathtaking countryside and perfect weather, with her wedding coming up in just a few days back in England. Yet she was desperately unhappy because it was clear to her that Dante would never love her the way she wanted him to. Suddenly she needed to be out in the open breathing in some different air.

'I will go for a drive with you if the offer is still open,' she announced, getting to her feet.

His mouth splitting into a satisfied grin, Alessandro made an extravagant gesture of waving her back into the house ahead of him. '*Signorina*, it will be my honour to take you for a drive.'

With the warm wind flowing through her hair, hurtling down the winding Italian country roads in Alessandro's outrageously flashy red sports car, Bliss told herself she truly was in another world. But, although the pleasure she derived from the experience was not to be discounted, she also knew that displays of wealth and its trappings did not impress her particularly. It certainly wasn't what she longed for the most. Since she had became pregnant with Dante's baby, a new longing had stolen into her blood—one that was seriously starting to consume her. What she craved more than anything else was having Dante tell her that he loved her and mean it. Then and only then could she go through with this intended marriage of theirs with any sense of doing the right thing. But as it wasn't likely that Dante would make such a declaration—even on their wedding day—Bliss would have to resign herself to marrying a man who she knew didn't love her and probably never would. Could she make such a mighty sacrifice for the sake of her unborn child?

'What do you think, huh?'

Shouting to make his voice heard above the engine noise, Alessandro stole a glance at the dark-haired beauty beside him, obviously eager to impress—both with his driving skills and his access to such an expensive toy.

'I think you're driving a little too fast for my liking,' Bliss shouted back, her stomach rolling over at the sudden acceleration in speed—particularly when they were on a very narrow strip of road curving into a hillside. She had a sudden vision of them careening into that hillside and that being the end of that. No more anguished decisions about whether marrying Dante di Andrea was the right thing to do or not. Her teeth clamped down hard on her lip. 'Slow down, Alessandro! You're driving much too fast!'

'Speed is an aphrodisiac, no?' Laughing into the wind, Alessandro made no effort to lessen his speed. The knot in Bliss's stomach turned into a sudden knifing pain that almost took her breath away. Shocked by the severity of it, Bliss went quiet. When it was followed by another slice of agony almost more severe than the first, she grabbed Alessandro's arm to get his attention.

'Please! You've got to stop!'

'Why? I cannot believe you are not having fun.'

'Oh, God…' Panicked by the now relentless waves of pain that were rolling through her body, Bliss knew she had to get Alessandro to turn the car around and take her back to the villa—either that or the nearest hospital. Whatever their destination, she was definitely in need of help. 'Alessandro, please!'

She finally got his attention. Seeing the colour drain from her lovely face, Alessandro narrowed his gaze in concern and started to slow his speed. 'What is wrong? Are you ill?'

'I think it's the baby,' she replied desolately, her violet eyes shimmering with tears. 'I think I might be losing it…'

Dante yelled at the hapless nurse who enquired what relation he was to Signorina Maguire, then swore at the doctor on duty who had attended her because he refused to give him any information on her condition until he received confirmation of the tests he'd run. In a cold sweat, Dante sat in the waiting room sightlessly staring at white clinical walls decorated with posters warning of the dangers of smoking, drinking and taking drugs, feeling as if he had had an argument with a ten-ton truck and come off the worst.

At first when he'd received an urgent telephone call from his mother, he had naturally thought that something had happened to his father. When Isabella told him that Bliss was in hospital suffering with severe stomach pains after being taken out on a drive through the countryside with Alessandro, Dante wanted to put his no-good cousin through the floor and bury him. He had made the forty-eight-kilometre drive from Milan at breakneck speed to get to Varese, his heart beating so wildly inside his chest that he could scarcely tell if he was breathing at all or simply surviving on the good will of God. If Bliss lost the baby, it would be his fault. He should never have left her. The business matter that had seemed so urgent when he had been back at the villa was not even akin to a speck of dust in his view now—let alone millions of dollars—in comparison to what was happening to Bliss.

Putting his head in his hands, he groaned, murmuring a heartfelt prayer, feeling as sick inside as if he had had poison injected into his blood. He had held onto the idea of his child since the moment he had found out Bliss was pregnant. Until that time he had had no idea how much he had secretly longed to be a father—to be important to someone in his own right. Now there might not be a baby after all and what reason would Bliss have for wanting to stay with him after that?

'Signor di Andrea? I am Angelo Berticelli, the head

medico on duty. I believe Signorina Maguire is soon to be your wife, yes?'

Already on his feet, Dante nodded dry-mouthed at the man who entered the room. 'How is she? I must be allowed to see her!'

He had to get her out of this poorly equipped state hospital and into the private one his family used as soon as possible, his thoughts ran on. He would get her the best care money could buy. But why had Sandrine not picked up on the problem when she had examined Bliss? Now Dante feared he had been wrong to trust the woman who was a family friend. If only there were the remotest chance that they could save the baby…he would do anything…*anything*.

'I have taken the liberty of contacting the chief obstetrician to come in and examine Signorina Maguire. Even though we have run some tests, we need his expertise. He should be with us within the next half an hour or so. Until then we have given the patient a sedative as she was somewhat agitated when she came in.'

Agitated? The possibilities that represented made Dante almost blanch. Did he mean that she was in great pain? He couldn't imagine the mostly serene young woman he knew making a fuss just for the sake of it. *Santo cielo!* She must be so frightened. All his muscles tightened as if the whole world were going to come crashing down upon him and smash his body into bits.

'Has she lost the baby?' His gaze was haunted as he asked the question.

'I am afraid I cannot tell you that, Signor di Andrea. You may speak with the obstetrician once he has examined Signorina Maguire. Please wait here and I will get a nurse to inform you the moment he arrives.'

'I cannot just wait here and do nothing!' Dante threw

his hands up in the air, for once in his life feeling powerless and useless. It was not a feeling he welcomed, nor ever wanted to experience again, not in this lifetime.

'I am sorry, Signor di Andrea, but you are going to have to do just that.' With an apologetic smile, the rather portly middle-aged doctor turned and left Dante alone.

CHAPTER TWELVE

BLISS'S head felt so thick and heavy that trying to think was like attempting to find her way home through fog with a blindfold on. As she struggled to open eyelids that appeared to have become weighed down with lead since falling asleep after the obstetrician's examination, she nevertheless registered the startling fact that the frightening pain in her abdomen was no more. What did it mean? Suddenly panicked, she tried to sit up. Had she lost the baby? Was that why she no longer felt any pain?

'What do you think you are trying to do?'

The sight of Dante approaching the hospital bed, the smooth, clean lines of his face now appearing pinched and drawn—haggard almost—so surprised Bliss that she automatically slumped back against the pillows. At this moment it seemed wise to surrender the battle of trying to hold her head up when it felt almost too heavy for her shoulders.

'I didn't know you were here.' Her lips were dry as sand and she longed for a drink. On the edges of her consciousness she wondered if Dante had been told she'd lost the baby and was wondering how to tell her. The thought was akin to being forced deep into the centre of a dank, dark cave with not a chink of light, then being told to find her own way out. She had a tendency to suffer from claustrophobia; now icy dread threatened to suffocate her.

'Of course I am here. Did you think I would stay in Milan when I heard you had been taken into hospital?'

As his hungry, examining gaze roved across her pale, anxious features Dante badly wanted to hold her close and pour out all his grief and regret. But he knew he had to be strong for Bliss. In her thin hospital gown there was a vulnerability about her that tore at his heartstrings. She had suffered enough already and did not deserve to carry the burden of his anguish.

'I—I can't think about anything right now except that I need a drink.'

Without hesitation, Dante reached for the jug of water on the bedside locker and poured some into the plastic tumbler beside it. Sliding his arm around Bliss's shoulders, he helped her to sit up and take a sip. Amazed at how fragile her bones felt against the solid strength of his arm, he experienced a wave of distress so acute he knew he was not very far away from tears. Was it only because Bliss might have miscarried their baby that his feelings were stirred so profoundly? Dante didn't think so. His desire to take care of the woman he was gently supporting was so strong that he almost believed he could hold back the sky to stop it from falling down on her.

'That's better. Thank you.'

'You're welcome.'

Being protective was one thing—holding back the tide of emotion that threatened to engulf him was quite another. Dante resolutely clenched his jaw and helped Bliss to lie more comfortably back against the pillows.

'Dante…have you heard? Do you know…do you know anything?' If she didn't mention the word 'baby', then maybe her terror would subside and she would be able to think what to do. But what did a woman do when she was possibly losing or had already lost a longed-for baby? Did she just calmly walk out of the hospital doors and try to carry on as normal—as if the awful devastation that had occurred inside her could be put aside as easily as an old CD that she had tired of listening to? She'd lost both parents and had been alone for a long time. Now, just when it had seemed that she might—just might— have a real chance at some happiness in becoming a mother, that chance was being cruelly snatched away again.

'No, *amorina*. Right now there is nothing I can tell you. The obstetrician has done his tests and will come and see us soon. That is all I know.'

Bliss had never heard Dante sound so unremittingly desolate. In the midst of her own deep sorrow her natural tendency to offer comfort made her want to reach out to him.

'Dante…you can father other babies. You have your whole future ahead of you. I am sorry I—that I couldn't…' Her voice trailed off to a bare, ragged whisper.

He could not believe she was actually apologising to him for miscarrying their child…and what did she mean when she told him he could father other babies? Was she suggesting he do so with someone else? Was she already withdrawing from him, knowing that at the end of this episode in their lives she would walk away from him? No! The thought was simply too crushing to contemplate.

Because he was so hurt and angry Dante said the first thing that came into his mind.

'What did you think you were doing tearing off round the countryside with Alessandro in that damned car?'

As she registered the scarcely veiled insinuation with disbelief, shock cut a swathe through the fog of dread that had enveloped Bliss. 'You're not suggesting that I somehow caused this situation by going for a ride in the countryside with your cousin?' Her violet gaze was filled with horror.

'No doubt the young fool was driving too fast—scaring you to death, most probably! When I get my hands on him he will rue the day his *mamma* gave him birth!'

'No, Dante! You mustn't blame Alessandro!'

'You would stand up for such a pathetic excuse for a man?' His emerald eyes glinting like slivers of ice, he glared at her. 'Perhaps you would be happier having a relationship with my cousin, no? You obviously admire him so much!'

Distressed, Bliss couldn't make her mouth work to voice a single word. She was saved from struggling to do so when the door swung open and Dr Berticelli walked into the room with a nurse hurrying behind him.

'How are you feeling, *signorina*?' He narrowed his eyes as if making an assessment from her appearance alone. Trying to gather her wits, Bliss dared a glance at Dante's glowering expression before replying. 'I—there's no pain. Is it because of the painkillers you gave me? Does it mean that I—?' It was no good. She couldn't finish the sentence. Not when her question might be sealing her own unhappy fate and also not when she sensed Dante's deep disapproval and suspicion of her supposed interest in Alessandro.

'Your condition is stabilised, Signorina Maguire. You have not lost the baby but over the next few months you will have to have more rest than most first-time expectant mothers if you are to carry this baby to full term. Signor di Andrea, you must ensure that she does not overdo things. I will sign a release form and leave it at the desk and tomorrow morning you may take the young *signorina* home again. If you need any more advice I suggest you talk to your own obstetrician at home. I will also give you a letter for him explaining our findings. These things are often difficult to detect and they will no doubt keep a closer eye on her from now on.'

From beneath her long dark lashes, Bliss saw Dante make the sign of the cross and then tears of happiness were rolling helplessly down her cheeks before she could wipe them away.

'Thank God. Thank you, Doctor. I am so grateful for everything that you did.'

'You are welcome, *signorina*. That is what we are here for. Signor di Andrea? If you will just come to the desk and sign—' But before Dr Berticelli finished speaking, Dante rose up out of his seat and exited the room as if suddenly remembering something of vital importance. Bereft because he had not stayed to share the miracle that their baby was still safe, Bliss sank back against the pillows and sorrowfully turned her face to the window.

He was so overcome he did not know what to do first. Adrenaline was shooting through his body like a jet plane run amok, leaving him on an incredible high one minute, then sobering him with fear in the next. He didn't want to let Bliss stay in the hospital for one more night…he wanted her home. But fear and common sense combined dictated that he do as the doctor suggested and let her remain where she was to make sure everything was all right. She had been so close to losing the baby that Dante would not knowingly jeopardise the chance of keeping them both safe, but from now on he swore to himself to do everything in his power to ensure that she would have a restful and stress-free pregnancy. He would not allow anything or anyone to put Bliss or the baby at risk again.

His mind busy with plans, he went outside to ring his parents on his cell phone. When Isabella started weeping with relief at the other end, the dam inside Dante finally burst and, giving way to his own overwhelming emotion in a way that he hadn't done since he was a small boy, he cried openly too.

'Isabella is preparing a special meal for us tonight—just you, me and my parents. Are you up to that?'

'Of course.' Glancing up at him from beneath the rim of the straw hat that she wore to keep out the glare of the sun, Bliss wished he wouldn't keep treating her as if she were spun glass or something equally fragile and breakable. She might be recovering from the scare of nearly losing their baby, but she was tougher than she looked and she wouldn't be doing anything foolish to put herself at risk. But still, this enforced rest was not as simple as she'd hoped it would be. After taking care of herself for so long it wasn't entirely easy to relinquish the reins, no matter how much she told herself to be grateful for the opportunity.

And Dante might be tender of her welfare, but physically he seemed to be maintaining a deliberate distance. In the three days since she'd been home from the hospital there'd been no more delicious suggestions about going somewhere because he needed to be alone with her. In fact, he seemed to want to do the exact opposite—suggesting that they join Isabella and Antonio and any friends that came to the villa at the slightest inducement. His behaviour just confirmed to Bliss what she already believed to be true: Dante was only interested in the baby. Once the baby came, would she be relegated to mother and wife only, not lover or friend? The thought swept cruelly through her like the desolate sound of rain falling on a burnt-out building—too late to put out the fire.

'I am going out for a little while. Can I bring you anything back? Some magazines, a book…maybe some candy?'

Bliss shook her head. Then, before melancholy settled on her shoulders like an unwanted but familiar cloak, she glanced back at him with hope in her eyes. 'If you're going out, can I come with you? I'd love a drive somewhere.'

The question seemed to give him more trouble than it should. Finally, as he shook his head Dante's tightly controlled little smile wasn't even rueful. 'No. That would not be a good idea, in my opinion. Stay here and rest. I do not intend to be away for long.'

'Is yours the only opinion that counts around here, Dante?' Drawing her knees up to her chest in the sun lounger, Bliss irritably wrapped her arms around them. 'This is a beautiful place, but I'm beginning to feel a little like a prisoner wrapped in velvet. The doctor said I needed to rest; he didn't say I should never go out again.'

'In two days' time we are flying back to the UK to see Sandrine. She will have to keep a very close eye on you now, after all that has occurred. There is also our wedding to think about. I want to make sure you are fully up to the travelling before we go and have to deal with these things, so in the meantime you need to rest as much as possible. It is not a question of me telling you what to do, it is a matter of you using your common sense.'

'Are you suggesting mine is in short supply?' she shot back, her irritation threatening to explode into full-blown anger. Rather than irritate him, her petulant retort seemed to amuse him. Levelling his disturbingly sexy green eyes on her, he smiled. It was the first real smile he'd bestowed upon her in the longest time and Bliss basked in the sultry summer glow of it, her senses revelling in the intimate attention like a shaded flower leant towards a sudden glimpse of the sun.

'I can see that you are spoiling for a fight, but I am sorry, *piccola*, I am not.'

'Why? Because you're afraid I'm going to break or something if I dare raise my voice or do something vaguely normal?' Rising to her feet, she whipped off her sunhat and threw it onto the striped lounger, almost in defiance of using her common sense. With her hands on her hips, she glared at him. 'Where are you going? Why can't I come with you? Are you going to meet another woman? Is that why you don't want to take me with you?'

'You really think I would cheat on you, Bliss?' Disturbed beyond measure that she would even fantasise about such a thing, Dante directed his slow-burning gaze fully on her trim, sexy body in her red shorts and white scooped-neck tee shirt. A heavy, languid heat attacked the lower part of his body and made his heart race with desire. If she hadn't recently almost lost their baby, he would have spent every spare moment they had together making love to her. His treacherous body was on fire for her, for the opportunity to repeat what they had done beneath the chestnut trees just a few short days ago with even more abandon than they had surrendered to then.

'You are more than enough woman for me, *carina*. I do not need to go elsewhere to find physical satisfaction, and I hope you do not either.' His heart beating a little too fast at the memory of Bliss's quick defence of Alessandro, Dante hoped that she had no regrets about marrying him and didn't wish it were his foolish younger cousin she was marrying instead. Even if she did, he was going to hold her to this marriage if it was the last thing he did, and barring acts of God they were going to make it work—at least for the sake of their child.

Biting her lip, Bliss turned away and hugged her arms over her chest. She was blind to the wonderful view of lush green forest that the horizon presented in a shimmering haze. Her senses were immune to the scent of honeysuckle and jasmine that floated so seductively on the air and her skin numb to the warmth of the sun that caressed the places on her body where it was exposed. All she was aware of, all she *wanted* to be aware of, was Dante. If only he could see how much she loved him, if only he could love her back in the same unrestrained, risk-all way that was burgeoning in her heart, then they might have a chance of making this coming marriage of theirs really work.

'Don't pretend you care whether I am physically satisfied or not, Dante. Not when you haven't come near me since I came back from the hospital.'

'Do you think that's how I want things to be?' Taking her by surprise, he came up behind her and turned her to face him almost savagely. 'It is torture for me day and night not to have you in my bed! I only have to catch the smallest flavour of your scent on the air and I am aroused almost beyond bearing! But I will not jeopardise our baby's chance of survival with my own selfish needs, Bliss. Already I worried… I feared that day in the woods when we…when I—'

Hardly aware that his fingers were digging almost painfully into her bare upper arms, Bliss stared at Dante with shock and sorrow in her heart. 'You don't think that because we made love that it somehow almost made me miscarry? Oh, Dante!'

Now that his fear was out, the relief of releasing it was like being let out of jail. How could he have lived with himself if anything had happened to their precious child because of him? He'd already carried the burden of feeling responsible for his father's rift with his parents for too long, without taking on another psychological load that had the potential to cripple him.

'A man thinks many crazy things when something like this happens,' he confessed hoarsely, tenderly stroking Bliss's hair back from her forehead as he did so.

'You take on too much, my love.' Letting her fingers graze down his beautifully shaped cheekbone, Bliss felt her eyes sting with the ache of holding back her tears. Dante's anguish about the baby was almost too much for her to bear. A man that had that much love inside him for a child not yet born surely didn't deserve for her to walk away just because he couldn't fully commit his heart to her?

She sensed him grow very still in front of her, his emerald eyes boring into her with profound surprise.

'What did you say?' he challenged her, his hand now burning her shoulder with the full, wonderful weight of his touch.

'I said you take on too much. You can't be responsible for everything that happens all the time. We are all adults here making our own decisions. I'm sure your family would be devastated to think that you felt you had to be solely responsible for their welfare. I know how that feels, because from a little girl I assumed all my parents' worries. Little mother, that was me, always trying to fix everybody's problems and taking all the blame for their hurts as though they were my fault.'

Wanting to press her to learn if she had meant the endearment she had addressed to him, Dante kept silent, understanding that Bliss carried too much pain about her own past and feeling remiss that he had not tackled her about it before.

'Why did your mother take her own life?'

Startled by the question, Bliss released a short, ragged breath before replying, her eyes downcast as she was forced to confront the stinging memory. 'She used to sit for hours just staring out of the window with a particular look on her face—' The trauma of the recollection seizing her chest in a vice, Bliss stared at Dante with a fleeting glance of terror, then quickly glanced away again.

'What look? Tell me.'

'As if—as if she was waiting for someone to come and rescue her and take her away from all the pain. Impossible, of course, when all the pain was on the inside. Sometimes I don't think my mother understood what she was doing on the earth at all, you know? It was as if she believed she was here by mistake. She walked around in a world of her own with my father and me on the outside desperately trying to make contact. I was so scared something bad was going to happen. So scared…' Briefly lifting her head, Bliss found it excruciatingly difficult to accept the compassion she saw blazing from Dante's eyes as he absorbed the words that fell from her lips. She had never fully expressed her feelings about her mother's death with anyone before—not even her father. This was a first.

'The depression she suffered from just intensified over time. The doctor gave her tranquillisers and anti-depressants and eventually she just withdrew into herself completely. My dad didn't know how to handle it. He loved her so much and it was killing him to see her like that so he turned more and more to drink to dull the pain. The week leading up to my mother's suicide, she suddenly became very animated and interested in what I was doing. I thought at first that it meant she was getting better…' Her throat feeling paralysed, Bliss sucked in a deep breath to try and anchor herself. Dante's hands tightened a little on her arms. 'I think what had happened was that she'd already made her mind up what she was going to do. Suddenly showering me with attention was her way of saying goodbye to me.'

'*Santo cielo!*' When Dante would have impelled her into his arms, Bliss deliberately resisted. Now that she was talking about things at last, she didn't want to stop until she'd finished. She hoped it would be cathartic if nothing else, even if she suspected that it wouldn't.

'She died after taking an overdose. Took so many damn pills her body must have been rattling before she— before oblivion hit.' Her brow contorting with grief, Bliss realised she was trembling hard. 'After—after she was gone…my father just seemed to give up on everything. I tried to get through to him, but he acted like I wasn't even there. I spent my time going through the motions of a supposedly normal existence when basically I was so frozen inside I would have been immune to someone putting a dagger in my heart. There was nothing I could do to help him. Our little family was beyond fixing by then…not even a miracle could save us. And so when I found the note he left that day when I came home… I'd be lying if I said it hit me like a ton of bricks. I guess I'd been expecting it.'

'And there was no one else around who could help you find him?'

Shrugging her shoulders resignedly, Bliss stared for a moment into space. 'I went to the police, but they told me they had so many missing people on their books they didn't hold out much hope. My dad left of his own free will and it was clear to them that he didn't want to be found. Made me feel about two inches small, that. Do you know how it feels to learn that your parents cared for you so little that one chose to commit suicide and the other would rather leave than stay in the same house as you?' She swore vehemently, anger as well as grief galvanising her. 'At least you know you are loved, Dante. I wish you knew how fortunate that makes you.'

When she would have torn herself free, her face threatening to crumple under the weight of emotion that was engulfing her, Dante held onto her fast—his expression grimly determined that she wouldn't escape before he said what he had to say.

'Things are different now, Bliss. It would not be true to say you are not loved.'

'I don't want you to think I am feeling sorry for myself.' She shuddered, trying hard to quell the almost unstoppable quivering in her lips with her fingertips. 'I don't know why I told you all that. It must have been the stress of nearly losing the baby that brought it on.'

'You are not listening to me, *amorina*.' Dante's beautifully shaped mouth looked almost tender as opposed to stern and Bliss gulped down a deep breath and wished she could just allow him to hold her for a very long time, at least until she was herself again. 'Did you not hear what I said about being loved? *I* love you, Bliss. My feelings for you have been growing stronger and stronger since our very first meeting. When you nearly lost the baby I almost wanted to die for your pain as well as my own. When I first saw you, so determined to hold onto little Renata until you checked out who I was to your own satisfaction—you were like a she-bear with her cub.' His gorgeous eyes crinkling at the corners, Dante's smile was wide and unrestrained. 'You impressed me then, *cara*, and you impress me even more now. I want a real marriage with you, Bliss. I am counting the days to our wedding…did you know that?'

Feeling as though she were in the midst of a dream, Bliss stared at Dante as relief, joy and profound shock poured through her bloodstream. He *loved* her? He really loved her? Dared she believe him? He wouldn't lie about something like that, would he? She tried to swallow across the lump in her throat, but could barely manage it.

'No… I—I didn't know that. I thought you were only interested in the baby.'

Her confession appalled him. His brow creasing in disbelief, he was immediately anxious to alleviate her fears. 'I think news of the baby just made me want you more, *cara*. I have waited a long time to have a family of my own, but I never seemed to meet the right woman to make my longing into a reality. Until you.'

'Are you sure, Dante?' Staring up at him as though she were frightened he might disappear before her very eyes, Bliss sighed. 'I don't want to be a burden to you— and I don't want you to feel in any way obligated to marry me because of the baby. That would be my worst nightmare.'

'No more nightmares, *tesoro*,' he said ardently and made a delicious shiver run down her spine. 'The reality is that I am honoured that such a beautiful, warm and compassionate woman has agreed to become my wife. I am marrying you because of my undying love and passion for you, my beautiful Bliss. And you can rest assured that I would have things no other way.'

'Now I'm happy.' Her lips curved into a delightful smile.

'And you called me ''my love''… Did you mean it, Bliss? I have to know.'

'Oh, yes, Dante. Of course I meant it! I love you. I think I will always love you...always!'

She let him pull her close then, her cheek resting against his heart as he stroked her hair and held her tight. 'And you don't prefer my cousin Alessandro?' Dante teased with a twinkle in his eye. Shocked that he would even jest about such an unbelievable thing, Bliss lifted her head and playfully thumped his shoulder.

'As if! There is only one man in this world that interests me, Dante di Andrea, and you know exactly whom I'm talking about. He's arrogant and gorgeous with a heart of gold, and I love him more than I love my own life.' She threw her arms around his lean, hard middle just because she could.

As he grinned with unashamed satisfaction at her possessive stance Dante's lips hovered just bare inches from Bliss's own.

'That is good. A man needs to know how his woman feels about him. *Ti amo*, Bliss. With all my heart...' No longer needing words to express how he felt, Dante kissed the woman in his arms as if his very life depended upon it, and, going by the whispers of need that she breathed against his skin between kisses, he wasn't being at all arrogant in believing she felt the same.

EPILOGUE

Eighteen months later

HE searched for her the moment he stepped out of the car, his senses led by the sound of laughter drifting on the air from the back of the house, on the *terrazzo*. Leaving his suitcase on the gravel drive, Dante resisted the urge to run and increased his already lengthy stride by conspicuous speed instead. He had been away on business in Lake Como for a week, helping Tatiana oversee the new extension that was being built on the now-thriving hotel she had taken over, and Bliss had been staying with his parents at their villa because Dante didn't want her to be alone. Now, he couldn't wait to see her again, to share the good news he had brought with his beautiful young wife and family.

'Dante!'

Standing beside his father, with little Roberto happily preoccupied on his grandfather's knee, Bliss glanced up almost as soon as Dante appeared round the corner of the house, her lovely face animated by unconstrained joy at his homecoming. Six months pregnant with their new baby, she was nevertheless shapely and fit in her white drawstring trousers and sleeveless blouse, her delicately tanned skin giving her a sultry, contented glow of well-being that made Dante want to steal her away from his parents and son there and then and show her in explicit detail just how much he had missed her.

He knew his parents wouldn't mind that he embraced

his wife first. But when their eager kiss lingered on into almost embarrassingly long seconds—his heart beating wildly at the fierce pleasure of holding Bliss in his arms—he wasn't surprised when Antonio had something to say about it.

'Ay ay ay! Let the poor woman draw breath, my son! Anyone would think that you had been gone six months instead of just one week!' Winking at his wife, who sat calmly beside him knitting for the new baby, he happily patted her knee. His own delight in his eldest son's happiness was clearly overflowing. 'And we are eager to hear your news. How is my darling Ana?'

'In love.' His lips parting in a helpless grin, Dante slid his arm possessively around Bliss's thickening waist and met her questioning gaze with a conspiratorial twinkle in his eyes. 'She has fallen in love with a young man named Raphael who is in charge of building the extension on the hotel. She spends most of her time gazing at him out of the window instead of working!'

'He must be very gorgeous, then.' Bliss smiled back into his eyes.

'I will ignore that remark until we are alone to-gether...then you will pay.'

Secretly thrilling at the deeply hungry and possessive tone in her husband's voice, Bliss playfully punched his arm and watched him go to little Roberto and swing him off his grandfather's knee, high into the air. Her heart did a triple somersault at the wondrous sight. She'd always believed that Dante would be the best father and in the past few months since their son's birth she had had ample evidence to support the fact. There truly could not be a more thoughtful, loving, patient, wonderful father on the planet. Except perhaps for Antonio, who day by day be-came more and more of a father to Bliss than her own troubled parent had been. And now they were going to have another baby to set the seal on their abundance of happiness. Bliss had been pronounced one hundred per cent fit and healthy by her new doctor at the maternity clinic in Milan, and so the concerns she had had when she'd carried little Roberto had been thankfully absent for the most part. She had a lot to be thankful for.

'Go and change out of the clothes you have travelled in and rest for a little while,' Isabella told Dante, rising to her feet. Nodding her head lightly in Bliss's direction, she smiled lovingly at her tall, handsome son. 'Take your wife with you. If I am not mistaken, she could do with a rest as well. Don't worry about little Roberto. *Papà* and I will take care of him until you come back.'

'*Grazie.*' Kissing his mother on the side of her cheek, Dante couldn't deny the leap of anticipation that shot through him at the idea of being alone with Bliss for a while. Returning his son to Antonio's willing arms, Dante caught his wife by the hand and led her into the house. Pausing outside the bedroom door, he cupped her face between his hands and as his dancing green eyes blazed back at her with love and adoration in equal measures he silently thanked God for bringing this priceless treasure into his life.

'You are not too tired?' he enquired a little anxiously, glancing down at the perfect little bump beneath her clothes. For answer, Bliss boldly reached behind her and opened the door with ill-concealed impatience in her hungry gaze. 'The journey from Lake Como must have addled your wits, Dante di Andrea! The day I don't leap at the chance of welcoming my husband into my bed will be the day the world comes to an end!'

More than gratified with such a reply, Dante gave her a playful little shove into the room and closed the door behind them.

MILLS & BOON®   0705/01b

Live the emotion

Modern
romance™

IN THE RICH MAN'S WORLD by Carol Marinelli

Budding reporter Amelia Jacobs has got an interview with
billionaire Vaughan Mason. But Vaughan's not impressed
by Amelia. He demands she spend a week with him,
watching him at work – the man whose ruthless tactics in
the bedroom extend to the boardroom!

SANTIAGO'S LOVE-CHILD by Kim Lawrence

Santiago Morais is strong, proud and fiercely passionate
– everything that Lily's husband was not. In his arms
Lily feels awakened. But a shocking discovery convinces
Santiago that Lily has betrayed him, and he sends her away
– not realising that he is the father of her unborn child…

STOLEN BY THE SHEIKH by Trish Morey

Sheikh Khaled Al-Ateeq has granted Sapphire Clemenger
the commission of her dreams: designing the wedding
gown for his chosen bride. Sapphy must accompany the
Prince to his exotic desert palace, and cannot meet his
fiancée. Sapphy doubts that the woman even exists…

THE LAWYER'S CONTRACT MARRIAGE
by Amanda Browning

Samantha Lombardi loved barrister Ransom Shaw. But
she was forced to marry another man to save her family.
Six years on, Sam is widowed and reunited with Ransom.
The sexual pull between them is still strong, and a red-
hot affair ensues. But will Ransom's desire be so easily
satisfied…?

On sale 5th August 2005

*Available at most branches of WHSmith, Tesco, ASDA, Martins,
Borders, Eason, Sainsbury's and all good paperback bookshops*

Visit www.millsandboon.co.uk

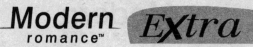

On sale 5th August 2005

*Available at most branches of WHSmith, Tesco, ASDA, Martins,
Borders, Eason, Sainsbury's and all good paperback bookshops.*

4 FREE

BOOKS AND A SURPRISE GIFT!

We would like to take this opportunity to thank you for reading this Mills & Boon® book by offering you the chance to take FOUR more specially selected titles from the Modern Romance™ series absolutely FREE! We're also making this offer to introduce you to the benefits of the Reader Service™--

- ★ FREE home delivery
- ★ FREE gifts and competitions
- ★ FREE monthly Newsletter
- ★ Exclusive Reader Service offers
- ★ Books available before they're in the shops

Accepting these FREE books and gift places you under no obligation to buy, you may cancel at any time, even after receiving your free shipment. Simply complete your details below and return the entire page to the address below. You don't even need a stamp!

YES! Please send me 4 free Modern Romance books and a surprise gift. I understand that unless you hear from me, I will receive 6 superb new titles every month for just £2.75 each, postage and packing free. I am under no obligation to purchase any books and may cancel my subscription at any time. The free books and gift will be mine to keep in any case.

P5ZED

Ms/Mrs/Miss/Mr ....Initials ....
BLOCK CAPITALS PLEASE

Surname ....

Address ....

....

....Postcode..

Send this whole page to:
UK: FREEPOST CN81, Croydon, CR9 3WZ